# NIGHT FLIGHT

## Sequel to  THE STOLEN YEARS

## by
# GLORIA REPP

Bob Jones University Press, Greenville, South Carolina 29614

**Library of Congress Cataloging-in-Publication Data:**

Repp, Gloria, 1941-
    Night flight / by Gloria Repp

        Summary: When a rift between her unsaved parents takes
    sixteen-year-old Kelly, a recent Christian, to a new home near
    the Pine Barrens of New Jersey, her faith in God is tested by the
    change as she tries to solve a mystery at the small airport there.
        ISBN 0-89084-563-8
        [1. Pine Barrens (N.J.)—Fiction.   2. New Jersey—Fiction.
    3. Christian life—Fiction.   4. Mystery and detective stories.]
    I. Title.
    PZ7.R296Ni   1991                                        91-116
    [Fic]—dc20                                                  CIP
                                                                AC

**Night Flight**

Edited by Mark Sidwell and Christa Habegger

Cover and illustrations by Cheryl Weikel

©1991 Bob Jones University Press

20  19  18  17  16  15  14  13  12  11  10  9  8  7  6

*For Jonathan,*
*who also loves the woods*

**Books by Gloria Repp**

*The Secret of the Golden Cowrie*
*The Stolen Years*
*Night Flight*

# Publisher's Note

Kelly Jonson, whom readers met in *The Stolen Years,* has been a Christian for only a few months. She has continued to grow closer to the Lord through her friendship with Nannette, an elderly French lady, and Dave Durant, whom she met at Nannette's cottage.

But Kelly's peaceful world falls apart when her father takes a job at an airport in New Jersey and decides that she must go with him. Upon arriving at her new home, she is dismayed at the peculiarities of her aunt and the two girls with whom she has to live, and she is worried about the alarming events that begin to occur in connection with her father's job. Besides the mysterious incidents at the airport, Kelly is troubled by the growing estrangement that she can sense between her unsaved parents. She suspects that her mother won't be joining them in New Jersey after all, and she feels betrayed when her father tries to hide what's happening. Her bitterness puts a distance between herself and God, causing her to doubt His love and her own salvation.

The testimony of a godly man helps her to understand that she can know God and trust Him better only as she talks to Him and reads His Word. She turns to the Lord with her problems, and when the time comes for her to make an important choice, she finds a true Friend and a solution to her dilemma.

# Contents

# Chapter One

# A White Box

Kelly Jonson slowed the downhill rush of her bicycle just long enough to swing off the road onto a gravel driveway. She shook back her wind-blown hair and scanned the house ahead of her.

David wouldn't be home this morning, but she'd had to come, just in case. It was her last chance to see him. *Last chance.* The words echoed through her mind as she slid from her bike and scrambled up the steps to the wide porch.

She knocked at the door, waited, and knocked again. No answer. For another minute she stood there, shifting from one foot to another, hoping that at least Susan, his sister, might be inside. Maybe back in the kitchen with Aunt Jeanne? But no footsteps pattered down the hall, and when she tried to turn the brass doorknob, it was locked.

Well, then–what about Nannette? Kelly hurried around to the back of the house, threw a farewell glance at the pasture behind it, and turned into the woods.

Nannette just had to be home. No matter what, she couldn't go without talking to her. *Last chance.* Kelly's feet thudded on the path, resounding in the peaceful green gloom. What was she ever going to do without Nannette?

Finally the trees thinned and she could see Nannette's white cottage. This early in the morning, she'd probably be in her garden. Kelly rushed down the stepping-stone path and around a corner of the cottage.

There she was, pruning a rosebush near the back porch. The tiny, white-haired lady looked around with a smile and waved her pruning shears. Then her bright gaze sharpened. "What's the matter, child?"

Kelly slowed down. Nannette could always tell.

"Sit here for a minute and talk to me," Nannette said, snipping off one last withered rose. Her calm voice reminded Kelly of all the times she'd come running to Nannette with a problem.

She sank onto the porch steps. "We're moving." The words seemed to choke her.

"You told me last week that your father was thinking about another job," Nannette said slowly. She put down the pruning shears. "So he has made up his mind?"

"Yes, all of a sudden." Kelly couldn't keep the bitterness out of her voice. "He's flying to New Jersey today and I have to go too."

Nannette frowned. "When was this decided?"

"It must have been last night. My parents were arguing like they always do, only it went on forever." Kelly paused, remembering how she'd buried her head under the pillow so she wouldn't hear the low, furious voices that came from her parents' room.

"Then first thing this morning, Dad told me to hurry up and pack because I was going with him." Slowly she added, "My mother didn't say a word all through breakfast."

"This job in New Jersey must be very important to your father."

"Yes, he's going to manage an airport near some little town called Harding." Kelly clasped her hands tightly around her knees. "I never thought he'd take the job because my mother is so set against moving."

Nannette nodded, and Kelly knew she understood. This wasn't the first time they had talked about Kelly's mother. "What is your mother going to do?"

"You know that lawyer she works for? He doesn't want her to leave. But after she trains another secretary for him, I guess she'il come to New Jersey."

Kelly jerked to her feet. "I can't stay–they'll be wondering where I went. But David's not home. I wanted to see him." It was hard to talk around the ache in her throat.

"Don't worry about David," Nannette said, standing up too. "I'll tell him and Susan what happened." She cocked her head and murmured, "You know, I think he's mentioned that town– Harding. Perhaps it's near where he used to live."

Kelly was only half-listening. "I just can't stand the thought of moving. How can Dad do this to me?"

Nannette stepped close and put an arm around her. "You'll do fine, Kelly. Be sure to take your Bible, and remember–I'll be praying for you."

"Thanks." Kelly hugged her and turned away. If she stayed for one minute longer, she'd be crying like a baby.

Quickly she retraced her path through the woods, back to her bike. Flinging a last glance over her shoulder at David's house, she pedaled down the driveway and turned toward home. As soon as she walked in the front door, her mother called from upstairs, "Where have you been, young lady?" Without waiting for an answer, her mother added, "You could have done this packing yourself. I wanted to get to the office early today."

"I'll finish it," Kelly mumbled, already on her way up the steps.

"Just fill up this suitcase–that's all," her mother warned. "Your father is loading the rest of your stuff onto the airplane. You'd better hurry and get cleaned up too. He'll be back soon, and I don't want him blaming me for anything else."

Kelly changed her clothes, made sure she'd packed her Bible and her bird books, and sat on the lid of the suitcase to close it.

She took one last look around the room, her gaze lingering on her collection of glass birds and the wildlife posters on the wall. Mother would have to bring them later, when she came. With a sigh, she lifted the suitcase off the bed, muttering, "I guess I'd better get back downstairs."

Her mother was waiting by the front door, already dressed for work. Her black hair was perfectly groomed, and she looked elegant in her navy blue suit. Impatiently she drummed long, polished nails against her purse. "I can't stay around much longer. Oh, here he is."

She gave Kelly a quick kiss and, surprisingly, a hug. "Now you take care of yourself," she murmured. "I'm sure you'll have a wonderful time." Kelly resisted a sudden impulse to cling to her. Instead, she stepped back, then followed silently as her mother hurried outside, leaving behind the faint scent of perfume.

Dad had just driven up to the house. He hunched his big frame out of the car, and the expression on his usually good-natured face was stern. Kelly tried to shrink into the background as her parents met on the porch. They hadn't said a word to each other all morning, and their silence worried her.

Her mother paused only for a second. "Good-bye, Bob; good luck," she said evenly and swept past him to her car.

He did not answer, but stared after her until she had driven away. At last he turned and saw Kelly standing in the doorway. "All set now?" He gave her a lopsided smile. "I'll take your bike apart, and then we'll be off."

When they reached the airport, Kelly's father stowed her suitcase and her dismantled bike in the back of their small, bronze-striped airplane and began his preflight check. She stood with the cool breeze whipping her hair, watching him and wishing that she were somewhere–anywhere–else.

"Kelly!"

She spun around at the sound of her name. A tall, dark-haired boy was running across the ramp toward them: *David.* Nannette had found him in time.

He skidded to a halt beside the airplane, his face worried. "You're really leaving?"

"Yes–" Kelly took a step toward him, wanting to explain, but there was no time. She glanced at her father; he was doing something in the cockpit. "Nannette will tell you."

"I already talked to her. Kelly–" He leaned closer, and she could see her own unhappiness mirrored in his brown eyes.

"Come on, let's go," called her father, still in the cockpit.

David seemed to change his mind about whatever he was going to say. He thrust a small white box into her hands.

"Remember Mr. Taylor?" he asked rapidly. "I was going to mail this to him, but he lives in Fairport, right near where you're headed. If you take it over, you'll get to meet him. Okay?"

"Sure." She clutched at the box. "David, I hope–"

"Kelly!" That was Dad again.

"I've got to go," she said. "Bye."

"Bye," David echoed. He stood there looking forlorn as she climbed blindly into the airplane.

# Chapter Two

# Trouble

Kelly yawned, fidgeting in the airplane's narrow brown seat. She flipped her book shut and nibbled at the peanuts that she'd bought when they refueled. It seemed like days since they had left Missouri, not just a few hours.

Usually she liked flying with Dad, but today the cities and farms and green valleys below made her think about all the miles that were rushing past. Every minute took her farther and farther away from the only real friends she'd ever had: Nannette and David and his little sister, Susan. Why did Dad have to insist on her coming with him, anyway?

Glancing at him, she was startled out of her resentment by the dark, brooding look on his face. He'd looked like that when they'd had the trouble with Bruce, her older brother. But now Bruce was off at school in Pittsburgh. Dad must be thinking about the problem with Mother. And he wasn't going to talk about it. Did he think Kelly couldn't tell that something was wrong?

All he'd been willing to say was that Mother would join them later, when things were settled. The vagueness of his answer made Kelly feel uneasy. What things? she wanted to ask. How were they to be settled?

The little plane hummed busily, as if trying to cheer her up, and a new thought consoled her. Maybe Dad wouldn't like this job and they'd come back to Missouri in a few weeks. She could pretend that this was just a vacation.

But a glance at the pieces of her bike, piled in the back seat of the airplane, sobered her. If this were just a vacation, Dad would never have let her bring that bike along.

Wondering where she might ride it, she ventured a question. "Where are we going to stay, Dad?"

He answered cheerfully enough, "You remember my half-sister, Jessica York? I guess you'd call her Aunt Jessica. She lives pretty close to the airport. I heard that her husband had died, but I hadn't seen her for years until I flew out last month to check on this job. That's when she offered to let me stay with her for a while. Until–well–until we see how things–um–work out."

Kelly wanted time to think about his words, with those odd blank spaces between them, but her father was hurrying on.

"Apparently she has two girls–sisters–living with her. Their parents were good friends of hers, and when both of them died, Jessica took the girls in. I guess they used to live in South America."

His voice tightened. "Jessica always was one for doing her duty. It's really very nice of her to invite us; so we'll have to try to get along the best we can."

Kelly started to ask about the girls, but he exclaimed, "Look out of your window. We're getting closer."

She leaned over and stared down at a wilderness so immense that it looked like an ocean, wind-ruffled and green. "Trees," she told herself in awe, "there's nothing down there but trees: hundreds and thousands of them." The vast dark forest, threaded with spidery white lines, stretched all the way to the blue haze of the horizon.

"You'd never expect to find something like that in the middle of New Jersey, would you?" her father asked. "It's called the Pine Barrens. See all the little white roads? People used to live there. I've heard stories about ruined towns hidden in those trees;

maybe we can hunt for some together.'' His eyes were sparkling now. ''And you'll see birds too–all kinds of them. The airport is right on the edge of the Pine Barrens; I think you'll like it, Kelly.''

He gave her a pleading glance. ''We're going to have a good time–just the two of us–aren't we?''

For his sake, she smiled, trying to ignore the ache inside her. ''How soon will we get there?''

''It won't be long.'' He checked the chart he had given her to hold. ''We should be able to see the airport right ahead of us.''

Kelly searched along a fringe of the pine woods and picked out a tiny runway next to three dots that must be the hangars. Beyond the airport, clusters of buildings huddled beside the curving ribbon of a broad highway.

''Yes, that's Harding all right,'' her father said, answering her unspoken question. ''Make sure you've got your seat belt on. We're entering the pattern.''

He radioed the airport and the plane glided down toward the runway. Kelly leaned forward; landings were almost as much fun as take-offs. She listened for the familiar beep of the stall-warning horn. A moment later came the chirp of rubber wheels on the pavement and then they were rolling smoothly toward the hangar complex.

As they taxied up to the ramp, a slender young woman hurried out to greet them. Kelly admired her long blonde hair and wondered who she was.

''Welcome to New Jersey, Mr. Jonson,'' the blonde girl said, smiling. ''I see you have a passenger.''

''Hi, Dina,'' answered Kelly's father. After introducing Dina, he explained, ''Dina does flight instructing for us and works in the office–''

He broke off as a white police car pulled up next to the terminal building. ''Why are the police here?''

Dina's green eyes looked uneasy. ''We just discovered that someone stole a radio from the radio shop. It looks as if the lock on the hangar was forced open last night.''

Kelly's father headed toward the terminal building and Dina followed, adding, "It was Mr. Biltner's radio, of all people. As soon as he found out, he insisted on calling the police."

Kelly hurried to keep up with them.

"Who is this Biltner?" asked her father.

"He's one of our biggest customers, but he's always unhappy about something," replied Dina. "Of course we'll replace his radio, but he'll never let us forget this."

They pushed through large glass doors into the airport waiting room. Kelly hung back while her father strode to the center of the room. A young policeman stood there, talking to a tall, black-haired man.

At the other end of the room, a group of men lounged around the coffee maker, and Kelly decided that they were probably pilots. Conscious of their stares, she slid into a chair beside the counter where Dina was working. A short, expensively dressed man stepped up to her father and began talking in a low voice. That must be Mr. Biltner.

"Would you like something to drink, Kelly?" Dina smiled and leaned over the counter with a can of soda.

She took it with an answering smile, grateful for Dina's friendliness, and settled back in the brown vinyl chair to wait. Sipping the soda, she watched her father as he listened and nodded; then he spoke quietly to the man. He seemed to have taken control of the situation, for the man was nodding in agreement.

As the men kept talking and the minutes dragged by, her mind wandered to the girls who were living with Jessica York. Dad hadn't said how old they were, but maybe they'd be teen-agers too, and at least she could make friends with them. Her stomach rumbled hungrily. Had he forgotten about supper?

Finally the policeman and Mr. Biltner left, and the curious pilots drifted away, one by one. "How about something from that sandwich machine for us, Dina?" Kelly's father said, bringing the black-haired man over to the counter with him. "Steak sandwiches okay with you, Kelly?"

She nodded, feeling shy under the tall man's dark, searching gaze.

"I guess you haven't met Mr. Carbonell. He's our chief mechanic," her father said. "Luis, this is my daughter, Kelly."

Luis Carbonell nodded solemnly at her. His tanned face was heavily lined, and now that she was closer, Kelly could see streaks of silver in his smoothly combed black hair. He glanced at his watch. "I have something to finish in the hangar, Mr. Jonson, if you will excuse me." His voice was deep and courteous, with a slight foreign accent.

"Sure," Kelly's father answered. "I'll see you tomorrow." The bell on the sandwich machine pinged, and he turned back to the counter, pulling some money from his pocket. Kelly helped him carry the sandwiches over to a round table in the corner where the pilots had been sitting.

They ate quickly, and as soon as her father finished, he stood up. "Guess I'd better phone Jessica," he said with a sigh.

Before long, a gray compact car drove up to the building; Kelly followed her father as he hurried out to meet it. A small, gray-haired woman stepped from the car and gave them a tentative smile. "Well, Bob, here you are at last. I was wondering what had happened to you."

"Yes, we made it. Looks like everything's all set." He sounded cheerful, but Kelly recognized the false heartiness in his voice.

Jessica York looked up at him with a worried frown. She flickered a glance at Kelly. "So you decided to bring her along after all? I suppose she can sleep with Eva; Tamara's room is much too small."

Kelly's father nodded. "We appreciate it, Jessica." He turned to pick up a suitcase. "Well, I guess we'd better get going."

The woman surveyed their pile of luggage. "Do you think you can get all of this into my car?"

"We'll sure try," he answered. "Give me a hand, Kelly." Silently she helped him stack their suitcases and the pieces of her bike in the car, and soon they were driving down the highway.

From her corner of the back seat, Kelly studied the lines on her aunt's narrow face and decided that she must be quite old. Her high, cool voice pattered on and on, filling the little car with comments about the weather and the airport and the town of Harding. She didn't exactly seem the type who'd welcome you with cookies and tea. . . . Kelly bit her lip, realizing that she'd been comparing the woman to Nannette. She glanced at her father. He was staring into the dusk with a resigned expression on his face.

At last they turned onto a cobbled driveway and stopped in front of an old-fashioned white house with tall black shutters. At one side of the house rose a tower with a pointed roof, dark and mysterious-looking in the twilight. It's like a castle tower, Kelly thought. She got out of the car and eyed it with a stirring of curiosity that was quickly drowned in a deluge of words from Jessica York.

"Now, Kelly, you'd better come right on up and meet Eva. I don't expect she'll feel much like sharing her room with you, but that can't be helped, can it?"

The woman went on talking, and Kelly, worried now about Eva, trailed after her father up onto a wide, white veranda.

"Where do you want these suitcases, Jessica?" Dad's voice boomed through the prim quiet of the house.

"You might as well carry them upstairs. I'll show you." Kelly's aunt led them up a polished staircase. "Bob, you can take the first bedroom, here."

She went on down the hall, paused to knock at a closed door, then flung it open. "This is Eva's room."

The girl inside did not look up. She was bent over something at a desk in the middle of the room, and all Kelly could see of her was a rough tangle of long brown hair.

Kelly's aunt hesitated, sniffing at the odor that hung in the air. "Eva, it smells awful in here," she complained. "You're always up to something." She bustled to a sofa bed in one corner of the room, pulled it open, and began tucking sheets into place.

Slowly the girl raised her head; the long hair fell back, revealing a pale, intent face. She kept her eyes on her work, and

Kelly watched curiously as she added the last touches of pastel green paint to one of the butterfly shapes in front of her.

Jessica York spoke over her shoulder. "I wish you would listen to me, Eva. You have a guest here." She finished the bed, still talking. "This is Kelly. You'll have to share your room with her for a while."

Eva picked up one of the butterflies and studied it. Life-sized and made of wafer-thin wood, it looked as fragile as a real butterfly. "Thank you, Mrs. York," she answered coolly. "I'll take care of Kelly. Maybe I'll introduce her to Brutus."

Jessica York's mouth tightened. "Make sure you clean up this mess," she said, and hurried out of the room.

After the door closed, Eva shrugged, murmuring, "Don't mind her. Always has to fuss and fidget about something." She stood up, a tall girl about Kelly's age, and began hanging the butterfly shapes from a wire arrangement suspended in the window.

"Those butterflies will make a pretty mobile," Kelly ventured.

Eva shot her a scornful glance. "They're moths. Luna moths. See the eye spots?"

Kelly had missed the black and yellow dot on each delicate green wing and the distinctive, curving shape of the back wings. "Yes, of course," she said. "I know what Luna moths are." She sat down heavily on the sofa bed; something was giving her a headache.

"What *is* that smell?" she muttered.

"It must be the paint," answered Eva. "I'll open a window if it bothers you. I'm almost done."

"Thank you," Kelly murmured. She sat silently, inhaling the cool evening air and watching the girl adjust the wires of the mobile. Eva seemed to have forgotten that she was even there. Finally Kelly stood up and fumbled through a suitcase for her pajamas. Before anything else happened, she was going to get some sleep.

And she was going to forget about that fussy old lady who was so different from Nannette; forget how far away she was from David; forget that it was Dad who had brought her to this strange, unwelcoming place.

Tomorrow she'd have to figure out what to do about it.

# Chapter Three

# New Faces

When Kelly awoke the next morning, she heard a faint tapping sound. It came from the mobile that Eva had finished last night and hung in the window. Kelly rolled over to watch the pale green butterflies twirl in the breeze. Moths, she corrected herself. Luna moths. She glanced at Eva's empty bed and sighed. If there was a chance of making friends with the girl, she'd better get that straight, at least.

As she dressed, she gazed around the room, which was crowded with dark, old-fashioned furniture and strewn with clothes. Despite the clutter, it seemed strangely impersonal, giving no hint of Eva's private interests. Even the remnants of last night's painting had disappeared, leaving the plain wooden desk top empty.

Besides the mobile, the only decorative item in the room was a large framed picture above Eva's bed. It seemed to be an assortment of butterflies. Kelly stepped closer. The butterflies weren't pictures. They were real, carefully positioned under the glass and set against a white background. Their wings, veined with delicate black tracery, glittered like jewels: sapphire, turquoise, and emerald.

Beautiful, Kelly thought. And decidedly tropical. David would love them. His name came unbidden to her mind, and with it, a tug of longing. She left the room and started downstairs, still thinking about him. If only she'd had time to say a proper good-bye, he might have promised to write her. Why couldn't Dad have let her come to New Jersey later on, with Mother?

She headed for the front door, stumbling through a living room that was still darkened by closed draperies, and stepped outside. Baskets of lacy green ferns swung at the edge of the wide verandah, and sunshine glistened across its floorboards. As she strolled over to the neat white railing, something behind her creaked. She turned quickly toward the sound.

A young girl with curly brown hair was watching her from a porch swing at the other end of the verandah.

Eva's sister, Kelly thought, maybe twelve years old. What had Aunt Jessica called her? Tamara.

The girl returned her gaze with a curious stare from wide brown eyes. Kelly smiled. "Hi, you must be Tamara."

The girl flushed under her tan. "I hate that name," she retorted. "My name is Tommie and don't you forget it." She jumped off the swing and stalked down the verandah with the ends of her shoelaces flapping. At the doorway she almost ran into Kelly's father, who was just coming out of the house.

He gave her a surprised glance as she ducked past him; then he turned to Kelly. "I'm glad you're up. Let's get out of here, and I'll treat you to breakfast. Jessica is lending me her car for the morning."

While Kelly ate her pancakes, she studied her father's face. He didn't look nearly as gloomy today. Maybe he'd feel like talking. She circled her fork through a pool of blueberry syrup and tried a leading question. "Could we bring Mom here for breakfast? Don't you think she'd like this restaurant?"

A gray, pinched expression touched her father's face, and Kelly waited uneasily as he mumbled something into his coffee cup.

He still doesn't want to talk about her, she told herself. There's something wrong, and he's trying to hide it.

Quickly she asked, "Could you put my bike back together for me today?" When he nodded, she hurried on, "And may I go out to the airport with you this morning? I didn't really get a good look at it last night."

Now he smiled. "Sure. No reason why you can't." He pushed his chair back from the table, as if eager to be on his way.

When they reached the airport, Dina was already making coffee. Her cheerful greeting seemed to brighten the waiting room, and Kelly gazed around it with interest.

Behind the counter was the desk where Dina worked on flight schedules and handled the telephone and radio; just past it was her father's private office. He invited Kelly in to see it. While she glanced over the repair manuals and technical books on his shelves, he began working at his desk. Before long he seemed to have forgotten about her.

A pilot's voice crackled over the radio, saying that he was going to take off, and she went back to the waiting room to stand at the wide windows. A small red-and-white Cessna was taxiing down the runway. Dina looked up from the desk with her ready smile. "Well, how do you like New Jersey so far? Do you know anybody around here?"

"Not in Harding," Kelly answered, "but maybe in Fairport–is that close by?"

"Yes, it's just down the highway from us. Are you going to go visiting today?"

"Sort of." Kelly hesitated, but Dina's friendly interest was hard to resist. "I have a box to deliver there."

"Secrets, huh?" Dina drew her eyebrows together, nodding mysteriously, and Kelly had to smile.

Dina looked at her with approval. "That's better. Those bright eyes of yours are so pretty when you smile. Why don't you go explore the hangar? It's right through that door at the end of the waiting room."

Kelly saw the boy as soon as she pulled the heavy metal door open. He was bending over an airplane on the other side of the hangar, and he looked so much like David that she caught her breath. He was tall, and his dark hair was short and curly at the back like David's–but no–it couldn't be.

The hangar door swung shut with a clang and the boy glanced up at her, his tanned face expressionless. No, of course it wasn't David.

She turned away and sauntered through the hangar, pretending to admire the airplanes and scolding herself for letting her imagination run wild. Off in the corner sat a boxy-looking, dark red plane that she recognized as a Stinson. As she started toward it, her foot hit something with a clunk. A paper cup flew into the air, and screws rolled in all directions.

Too late, she saw that the airplane next to her had its cowling off. Someone–probably that boy–must have put the screws in a cup to keep them together. She felt her cheeks flame with embarrassment. Awkwardly she scrambled across the concrete floor to pick up the screws, hoping that the boy hadn't noticed.

But he had. She knew it as soon as she stole a glance in his direction. Why did he have to stare at her with that annoyed look on his face? He probably thought she was a clumsy idiot, but he should have put that cup of screws farther back under the airplane in the first place. Dad always did.

Before the boy could say anything, she dumped her handful of screws into the cup and headed for the wide-open front of the hangar. She crossed the ramp, slipped past the corner of a smaller hangar, and paused at the edge of a wide, grassy field. At least no one could stare at her now.

On the far side of the field, she saw her father's bronze-striped Cessna, tied down beside several other small planes. From this distance they looked like a flock of brightly colored metallic birds that had been tethered there to feed.

As she started toward them, she found herself thinking again about the trouble between her parents. What was the matter with them, anyway? Here she was, sixteen years old; why couldn't they at least tell her what was going on, instead of treating her like a baby?

She shook her head and tried to concentrate on looking around the rest of the airport. Beyond the field stood an old farm house half-hidden by trees, and behind it loomed a dark-crested wall of pines that must be the Pine Barrens. From what Dad had said, that might be an interesting place to explore.

She strolled past the planes and then returned to the small metal hangar, where she sat down with her back against its sun-warmed wall. The red-and-white Cessna was still practicing land-ings, and she grew drowsy as she watched it take off again and again. But anything was better than being left with Aunt Jessica and those two girls.

What would she do with herself this afternoon? Now was the time to make plans. As soon as Dad put her bike back together, she could take David's box to Mr. Taylor. Maybe he'd chat with her for a while about David, and then they could talk about birds. He'd know a lot about the birds in the Pine Barrens.

Last year, when David lived in New Jersey, Mr. Taylor had been his science teacher; David had told her that he was a fasci-nating character. Now she could find out what he meant.

"Kelly?" Her father's call interrupted her daydream. She jumped to her feet and trotted past the main hangar to the gas pumps where he stood waiting. "Oh, there you are," he said. "It's time to go on back for lunch."

"Lunch time already?"

"Yes. Well, Jessica said she always eats at eleven-thirty. So we'd better make sure we're there on time." As they got into the gray car, he added, "Jessica wants this back soon; so this after-noon I think I'll start looking for one of our own."

When they arrived, the long table in Aunt Jessica's dining room was already set with plastic placemats over a lace table cloth. The small room was crowded with furniture that looked very old and equally solemn. The two girls appeared and sat down silently. Kelly followed their example and managed to squeeze into a chair without bumping the antique buffet behind her.

They were half-way through the meal when Kelly remembered the stolen radio. Between bites of her ham sandwich, she asked whether the police had discovered who took it.

"The police are still working on the case," her father said. "I don't think they can do anything about it." Eva had paid no attention to the conversation, but Tommie gave them a quick, interested glance. "What about fingerprints?" she asked.

"There weren't any, it looks like." Kelly's father helped himself to a pickle and remarked, "That young policeman is really friendly, though. They call him J. L. He suggested that I put new locks on the radio shop and the hangar. They'll be dead-bolt locks–good and strong. I ordered them this morning."

"Don't leave any spare keys out at the airport," advised Aunt Jessica. "Maybe one of your employees stole the radio. I'd watch that tall, dark-haired one; I've heard he has a prison record."

Kelly listened curiously. Was she talking about Mr. Carbonell?

"Luis Carbonell seems quite trustworthy," her father said, sounding annoyed. "He used to live in Cuba, and if the Communists put him in prison there, it was probably just political."

When Aunt Jessica shook her head as if she were unconvinced, he added, "Don't worry about the spare key, Jessica. I'll probably keep it in the glove compartment of my car."

For the first time, Eva spoke up. "May we please be excused?" At Aunt Jessica's nod, the girls left the table, and Kelly watched them go, wondering why they'd been so quiet. Now her father had taken a last swallow of iced tea and was pushing back his chair. "I'd better get going too. I want to run over and look at a car I saw in town."

"But Dad, what about my bike?" exclaimed Kelly.

He was already on his way out the door. "Sure, I'll fix it; maybe tonight. See you later."

As she stared after him, her aunt said, "Kelly, you haven't unpacked yet. Your clothes will be all wrinkled, and I don't have time for extra ironing."

Kelly slumped in her chair. "Okay; I guess I might as well get it over with."

"That's not a very polite answer." Aunt Jessica gave her a reproving glance from frosty blue eyes. "I'd think you might be more considerate, Kelly. I really don't know why you young people have to behave so selfishly." She lifted her small pointed chin. "As I was telling the ladies in my sewing circle just the other day, I wish you teen-agers had manners like Phillip and Harold. They always treated me so nicely. Now get along and do that unpacking right away."

Kelly blinked at her aunt in surprise. She stood up, knocking a spoon onto the floor, and snatched it up, muttering, "Yes, ma'am; excuse me, please."

Before the woman could start in again, she hurried upstairs. How could Dad have such a dreadful sister? Half-sister, she reminded herself. And who were Phillip and Harold, anyway?

In the bedroom she found Eva sprawled across her unmade bed, reading. She didn't look up when Kelly came in; so Kelly tried to be unobtrusive as she opened a suitcase and began unpacking. She lifted out the white box David had given her and laid it carefully on top of the dresser.

It was a flat, rectangular box, only an inch or two deep and five or six inches wide. Probably it held some unusual insects that David knew Mr. Taylor would appreciate.

If only Dad had fixed her bike, she could have delivered the box this afternoon. Well, why not try putting the bike back together by herself? She had watched him take it apart. Yes! Her mind made up, she continued unpacking with more enthusiasm.

As she reached for the last suitcase, she realized that Eva was watching her over the edge of the book. To break the silence, Kelly asked, "Who's this Phillip and Harold that Aunt Jessica is so proud of?"

Eva heaved a dramatic sigh and imitated Jessica York's high voice, "Why, they're the sweetest, most wonderful boys that a mother could have."

"Her kids? Where do they live?"

"They're all grown up now–moved to California. Probably couldn't stand listening to her, but she still talks about them all the time. And she still keeps a bedroom ready for each of them."

The framed butterflies on the wall above Eva's head caught Kelly's eye. "I've never seen butterflies like that before, except in books. Did you press them yourself?"

"They were my father's," Eva said, suddenly cold and quiet. "From Brazil."

"You'll have to tell me what kind they are," Kelly mumbled, wondering what she'd said wrong this time. "I wish David could see them."

Eva sat up with a sigh of impatience and pushed the heavy brown hair away from her face. "Who's David?"

"He lives in Missouri, where I do. Where I used to live. He started working at the airport with my dad, just this summer." Kelly faltered, not wanting to admit how much she missed him. Finally she added, "David's crazy about all kinds of insects."

That reminded her of the white box. "Do you know anything about Fairport? David gave me a box to deliver to a man who lives there."

"Sure." Eva clipped a large barrette untidily in her hair. "What's his address?"

Kelly glanced at David's careful writing on the box. "It's 126 Birch Road."

"Okay, that's not very far away. Just take the highway into Fairport and you'll go right past Birch Road." She returned to her book.

"Thanks." Kelly opened the last suitcase and hurried through its contents. Shoes in the closet. Shirts in the drawer. A dress to hang up. Books. She added her Bible to the stack of books.

Eva glanced up. "Oh, wonderful; a Bible reader in our midst," she muttered. "You don't really believe that stuff, do you?"

"Yes, I believe it," Kelly said, hating the apologetic sound of her voice. She picked up two empty suitcases. "What am I supposed to do with these?"

"Put them down in the basement, I guess. Ask Tommie."

Kelly carried her suitcases out of the room, pretending to ignore the scornful expression on Eva's face. She heard a rhythmic *thump-thud* coming from the front of the house and found Tommie throwing a tennis ball against the spotless white walls of the living room.

"Does Aunt Jessica let you do that?" she asked in surprise.

"Nope, not when she's here," Tommie said without looking around. "What do you want?"

"Eva said you'd know where these suitcases belong."

Tommie made a diving catch before she answered. "Put 'em down in the basement, on the shelves by the washing machine."

"And I need a screwdriver," Kelly added.

"In the corner by the shelves. There's a chest with a bunch of drawers in it." Tommie swung around to give Kelly a brief stare. "Just be careful where you go wandering around down there, or you'll get in trouble with Eva."

Kelly decided not to answer that remark. She turned away, then stopped. A closed door set into an alcove between the living and dining rooms reminded her of the tower she'd seen last night. "Is this a closet or what?" she asked Tommie.

"Huh? Oh, that just goes up to the attic somewhere."

It might go to the tower. Kelly gave the doorknob a quick twist as she went by, but it was locked. Disappointed, she wandered into the kitchen and found the basement door.

She thumped down the narrow steps with her suitcases, hoping that her father had put the parts of her bike down here too.

Yes, there they were, lying beside the washing machine. And in the corner, just as Tommie had said, she found a tall, narrow chest that must have had a dozen shallow drawers.

The top drawer held an collection of dusty flashlights, and the next one was full of nails, neatly boxed. The third drawer had nothing in it but keys. Kelly poked at them curiously. There seemed to be all kinds and sizes–keys for trunks, for doors, for desks–and some of them looked as if they were a hundred years old. But they won't be much help with my bike, she had to remind herself, shutting the drawer reluctantly. At last she found a drawer with an assortment of small tools, and she picked out a screwdriver and a wrench.

Quickly she set to work on the bike, trying to remember how her father had taken it apart. As time passed, she realized that the project was taking a lot longer than she'd planned. There wouldn't be time to go today.

At least it will be all ready for tomorrow, she told herself. I won't have to wait for Dad. First thing, I'll take that box to Mr. Taylor.

Finally she had only the pedals left. As she picked up the first one, she heard someone coming down the basement stairs. It was Eva, carrying a handful of leafy branches. She stopped at the foot of the steps and gazed at Kelly without a trace of her former unfriendliness. "Come on, you've got to meet Brutus."

Kelly put down the bike pedal and eyed her doubtfully. She still wasn't sure what to think about this girl.

Eva walked over to the wood paneling that formed one wall of the basement room, pried out two nails, and slid a strip of wood to one side.

All Kelly could see through the hole was blackness. But Eva had taken out a flashlight. She looked back at Kelly. "You coming?"

Kelly had to admit that she was curious. She stepped through the narrow opening and waited in the gloom while Eva slid the panel closed behind them.

# Chapter Four

# Eva's Den

"It's this way," Eva said. She started off into the darkness.

Kelly kept close behind her, stumbling as the concrete floor changed to uneven stone slabs under her feet. The beam of the flashlight showed only a narrow passageway that twisted between stacks of boxes and shrouded furniture, but Eva seemed to know exactly where to go.

A minute later they reached a small wooden door. Eva put one shoulder to it and the door swung open. The square room in front of them was dimly lit by a narrow, curtained window, high on one wall. The other walls were covered with striped fabric: sheets, Kelly guessed, tacked in place at ceiling and floor.

She followed Eva across a faded green rug, passing an old armchair with a table next to it that held a battery-powered lamp and a stack of books. A pair of tall bookcases stood nearby, crammed with birds' nests, dried grasshoppers, jars of preserved cocoons, and displays of mounted butterflies.

Eva pulled aside the curtain, and a patch of sunlight fell on a long table under the window. On the table were several insect-killing jars, which Kelly recognized right away, and two medium-sized cardboard boxes, each with one end hinged like a door and covered with fine mesh.

Eva had opened the door of one box and pulled out a jar full of wilted branches. "Here's lunch, you guys," she said to the fuzzy orange and brown caterpillars that clung to the branches. Replacing the old branches with fresh ones, she deftly transferred the caterpillars and shut the door of the box, turning it toward the light.

"Now you've got to meet Brutus," she said. "Here in the window."

Kelly leaned across the table and looked up at the dusty windowsill. In a corner, half-hidden by the curtain, crouched a large yellow spider with black markings on its bulging abdomen. Eva threw Kelly a sidelong glance. "This is Brutus."

She stood still while Brutus glared at her with yellow eyes. "Oh, yes," she said, trying to sound indifferent. "David showed me a spider like that once, but I forget what he called it. How come you've got him in here?"

"Brutus keeps Mrs. York out of my way; she's terrified of spiders." A wry smile twisted Eva's lips. "She never bothers me down here."

"But what does he eat?" asked Kelly.

"I bring him flies and we get along fine."

Kelly stepped back and waved at the other box. "What've you got in there?"

"A Catocala moth. I'm waiting for her to lay some eggs."

Kelly wanted to ask about the butterflies she could see pinned to a spreading board, but Eva cocked her head. "Sounds like Tommie's stopped bouncing her ball; so the lady of the house must have returned." She picked up her flashlight and jerked the curtain closed. "We'd better get back upstairs or she'll start asking questions again."

Kelly managed to follow Eva's swift retreat without stumbling, but she bumped into dusty objects at every turn of the passageway.

"How did you ever find that room, anyway?" she asked, rubbing an elbow.

"Oh, I was exploring one day, and there it was. It probably used to be an old wine cellar, but now it's my Den. I fixed it up myself. I don't think Mrs. York even knows it's back there. This house is really ancient."

When they stepped back into the main part of the basement, Kelly could hear Aunt Jessica's heavy footsteps on the kitchen floor over their heads. Hurriedly she stood her bike up and adjusted the kickstand.

A minute later the door opened. "Eva? Kelly? What are you doing down there?"

Eva picked up a screwdriver, answering smoothly, "I'm just helping Kelly with her bike."

They trailed up the stairs toward Kelly's aunt. "Look at you girls!" she complained. "Kelly, you're filthy. There's dirt all over you, and you're tracking it into my kitchen. Eva, you've been up to your secrets again, and I don't like it."

Kelly brushed at her dusty blouse in surprise. That must have happened when she ran into those things in the dark. She wiped up a few specks of dust from the floor and hurried upstairs to change. Maybe Aunt Jessica would calm down by supper time.

But when Kelly's father arrived an hour later, Aunt Jessica was still talking about it. She made a point of remarking that Kelly really should learn to keep herself more tidy.

He frowned tiredly as he listened. While they walked together into the dining room, he muttered, "Please, Kelly, try not to be a problem."

She pulled away from him and sat down at the table. At least Dad could have asked her what had happened. He always used to.

She stared at her plate. Aunt Jessica's tuna casserole didn't smell very good. She stabbed at the slippery mass with her fork and took a cautious bite. Glue. Fish-flavored glue, she decided. She ate it anyway, wanting only to finish the meal quickly so that she could get away from the table, away from everybody. If only she had a place where she could go to be alone! Eva had her Den to escape to, at least.

After supper, Kelly wandered restlessly from the living room into the small, book-lined room that Aunt Jessica called the library. A cushioned seat in the deep bay window looked inviting. She curled up there and gazed soberly at the skyline, where pine trees were outlined in jagged black against the golden sunset. A minute later she felt someone squeeze in beside her.

Tommie's voice was hushed. "Looks spooky out there, doesn't it? Have you heard about the murdered man who wanders along the creek banks at night, swinging his lantern?" She chuckled, sounding agreeable for a change. "They say Captain Kidd buried his treasure somewhere in the Pines too."

Kelly put on a skeptical face, but Tommie added eagerly, "There's lots of ghost towns hidden out there; that's a fact. I think that's where the treasure is. And some folks talk about the Jersey Devil like he's still hiding in the cranberry bogs."

"Well, you're full of tall tales, aren't you?" Kelly left the window and picked a book at random from one of the shelves.

"I thought you'd be interested," Tommie said cheerfully. "I know a lot of good stuff about the Pines. I'll tell you some more if you let me go out to the airport with you." Her voice had taken on a pleading note.

Kelly hesitated. So that was why Tommie had decided to be friendly all of a sudden. But she couldn't blame the girl for wanting to get away from Aunt Jessica.

"I guess Dad won't mind," she said at last. "How about tomorrow afternoon?"

"Great!" Tommie jumped up from the window seat and skipped away. The room seemed much too quiet after she had gone.

Kelly paged aimlessly through several books, wishing that she and her parents were settled in a house of their own. Or better still, that Dad would change his mind and go back to Missouri. Finally she chose a mystery story and took it upstairs with her.

Eva was sitting at her desk, pinning a yellow and black moth onto a spreading board, but she had dropped her butterfly net on Kelly's bed and left a pile of books in the middle of Kelly's dresser. Right then Kelly decided that she had to do something about this room, even though she was only staying for a few days.

"Eva," she said, "I've got to have part of the bedroom for myself. I'm going to move some furniture." She pushed her sofa bed into a corner and turned the dresser and bookcase around to form a room divider.

Eva watched her with amiable interest. "Take a chair and a lamp too," she suggested, standing up to survey the new arrangement.

Later that evening when the lights were out, Kelly wondered how she was ever going to get along with Eva. When she'd seen Eva's Den, she had thought that maybe they'd have something in common.

But Eva was so changeable! Although she seemed friendly tonight, this morning she'd been silent and irritable; and sometimes she just stood at the window doing nothing, a dreamy look on her face. She said she was the same age as Kelly, but she seemed older. Maybe it came from living in South America and traveling around so much. She certainly was a strange kid, whatever the reason.

Thinking about Eva's oddities sharpened the loneliness Kelly had been trying to ignore. She buried her face in the pillow. Nothing felt right any more, not since they'd left Missouri. It seemed as if she had left behind all the parts of her life that were warm and safe and good. Even Dad seemed different here.

She rolled over and settled the pillow firmly under her head. But there was tomorrow. She held onto the thought of David's white box. Now she was ready to deliver it; she could look forward to that.

After breakfast the next morning, Kelly put the box into her bicycle basket and set off toward Fairport with a light heart. It felt good to be biking again, with the wind lifting her hair and the tires whispering companionably beneath her.

The wide shoulder of the highway made for fast riding, and soon she was entering the small town. The street signs flew past so quickly that she almost missed Birch Road. It was a short street, lined with look-alike brown houses that had sharply peaked roofs. She parked her bike in front of #126 and peered through the glass on the door. Judging from the mail slots inside, the house had been converted into four apartments.

She stepped inside to check the names. None for Mr. Taylor. This couldn't be the right place. She was turning to leave when a door next to the staircase opened.

A plump face smiled out at her. "Who you looking for?" The woman's orange-flowered dress billowed into the dusty hall.

"It's Mr. Taylor–he's a teacher, and I–"

"Sure, he used to live here, but not anymore." The woman gave her a sympathetic look. "He's got a cabin in the Pines. Might try that." She chuckled, then added, "He usually hides out there until school starts. Don't want to see or hear nobody."

"Please, do you know where his cabin is?" asked Kelly. "I have to deliver something to him."

The woman glanced curiously at the box in Kelly's hand and scratched at her frizzy brown hair as if trying to make up her mind. "Well, okay. Just take the highway past the airport in Harding–you know where it's at?"

Kelly nodded eagerly.

"Oops! There goes that good-for-nuthin' bird."

Kelly ducked as a green and blue parrot flew heavily into the hall and perched on the banister of the stairway.

The woman hurried after the bird and put out an arm for it to step onto. The bird examined Kelly with one orange-rimmed eye and then let out a screech.

"Yes, Blue-Boy, we know how handsome you are," the woman said in a soothing voice. "Now calm down and get back where you belong." She left the door open while she carried the bird back into her room and shut him into a large cage.

"He's a beauty," exclaimed Kelly. "What kind of parrot is that?"

"Blue-Boy is a Blue-fronted Amazon." The woman's face shone with pride. "He's pretty smart too. Bought him down the street at Carl's Pet Shop, and he cost plenty. They got all kinds of birds in there. You like birds?"

"I sure do."

"Then you've gotta go look around at Carl's. He won't mind. Now where were we?" The woman glanced back at Blue-Boy, who was scattering seed hulls across the floor of his cage. "Yeah, after the airport, you take the next right–it's one of them little sandy roads. Keep turning right every time the road forks, and pretty soon you'll cross a creek. Then you go left. The other way goes to the fire tower."

Kelly thanked the woman and rode off in a hurry, hoping that she'd still have time to find the cabin this morning.

But while she waited impatiently for a traffic light to change, she heard the *pss-sh* of a tire losing air. She kicked at her flat tire and sighed, wishing she'd brought along the tire patch kit. Now she'd have to stop back at Aunt Jessica's before going to look for the cabin.

On her way down the sidewalk she passed the pet store that the woman had mentioned, and she paused in front of the window to admire a green and blue parrot that looked like Blue-Boy's brother. Inside the store she could see rows of colorful, chattering birds in cages. She'd have to come back when she had more time.

To Kelly's dismay, Aunt Jessica met her at the door of the house. "Why didn't you tell me where you were going, young lady? I can't have you running all over the countryside by yourself. What will people think? Now put that bike away." She must have noticed the protest on Kelly's face, for she added "Yes, you must. Then you may help Tamara finish up the kitchen cupboards before lunch time."

Feeling only slightly repentant, Kelly worked hard at scrubbing the kitchen cupboards, and she was glad to hear her father's booming voice at last. He must be home for lunch.

After they'd eaten, Tommie reminded her about going to the airport, and Kelly's father offered them a ride in the green station wagon he'd bought. Kelly ran upstairs to comb her hair and glanced regretfully at David's box, still sitting on the dresser. It would just have to wait until tomorrow.

On the way to the airport, she wanted to ask her father about the stolen radio, but he looked preoccupied; so she saved her questions for later. His only remark when they left the car was "Stay out of trouble, will you, girls?"

Huh, Kelly thought. Was that all he could think of to say?

Tommie wanted to see all the planes; so Kelly took her into the big hangar, hoping that they wouldn't run into that boy again. As they passed the door of the radio shop, however, Tommie caught sight of him and whispered, "Look who's there!"

"Well, who is he?" asked Kelly.

"That's Ron. Ron Carbonell! He plays on the high school basketball team. Oh, here he comes. I've got to talk to him."

She ran over to intercept the boy and Kelly followed, taking her time. When she got there, Tommie stopped talking long enough to flash her a smile. "He works here, Kelly. Ron works for your dad."

Before she could answer, Tommie had turned back to Ron. "I didn't know you could fix airplanes. Can you fly them too?"

"A little." His face lost its sober expression. "Are you going to cheer for us at the basketball games again this year?"

"I sure am. Oh, Kelly, you ought to see him shoot baskets. That's what I want to be, a basketball player."

"I thought it was baseball," Ron said with the trace of a grin.

"Yeah, that too." Tommie tossed her curly head. "Someday I'm going to be as good as you are, Ron."

He looked embarrassed and retreated toward the radio shop. "I'd better get to work, or I won't have any money to buy gym shoes next year."

"That's right," Tommie agreed. "Let's go."

As they left the hangar, Tommie chattered on about basketball games, and Kelly, half-listening, decided that the boy didn't look very much like David after all. His hair was curlier, for one thing, and his eyes were so dark that they were almost black. She wondered about the sadness that she could see in those eyes.

"What's over there?" asked Tommie, pointing across the field of airplanes.

"Just some old farm buildings, I guess."

"I love places like that," Tommie exclaimed. "Let's go look."

As they drew closer to the farmhouse, Tommie muttered, "It sure is old." Kelly nodded, thinking that it had a forlorn, neglected air, with its boarded-up windows and flaking white paint.

They skirted the sagging porch and pushed past a clump of hydrangea bushes that were heavy with purple blooms. A weed-choked driveway led from the house into the woods.

Tommie darted past the house toward a weathered barn that looked as closed-up as the house. "Hey, it's got a lock on the front," she called back.

When Kelly reached the barn, she found Tommie behind it, already climbing into one of its windows.

"What are you doing?"

"The nails were loose, and a board sort of fell off when I pulled on it." Tommie wore an innocent grin. "I just want to look inside."

She disappeared, and a moment later Kelly heard her delighted cry. "You've got to see this. There's a plane in here."

"What?" Kelly hiked herself up and squeezed through the window, dropping into a wide room that still smelled like musty hay. A small blue airplane took up most of the space. She examined it curiously in the dim light.

Although she recognized the high wings and tricycle gear of a Cessna 182, this one had five little curved plates sticking up from the top of each wing. Different. As she walked around it, she noticed the odd little fins on the nose of the plane. Mounted just behind the propeller, they looked like a pair of small, blunt wings.

"It looks funny," Tommie said, following her gaze. "Like the plane is wearing a moustache. What kind is it?"

"I don't know," Kelly said slowly. "I've never seen anything like it before–" She was interrupted by the wail of a siren.

Tommie headed for the window. "Let's get out of here."

Kelly scrambled after her with the siren ringing in her ears. They slammed the board back into place across the window and peered around a corner of the barn.

A yellow fire truck, its lights blazing and siren wailing, was hurtling up the airport drive.

# Chapter Five

# Mr. Taylor's Cabin

The fire truck halted behind the large hangar. "What's going on?" Tommie asked.

"Let's find out." Kelly started off through the field of airplanes, exclaiming in alarm when the wide hangar door went up and smoke billowed out. She broke into a run with Tommie close behind her and didn't slow down until they reached the ramp.

"There's Ron. Let's ask him." Tommie slipped past two firemen to reach Ron, who was standing beside the hangar looking angry.

He shook his head in answer to Tommie's question. Kelly heard him say, ". . . a smoke bomb in the radio shop. Who'd be dumb enough to pull a stunt like that?" Then he turned and disappeared into the smoky hangar.

"Wait!" Tommie ran after him, but a policeman stopped her at the entrance.

"Hey; watch it. You're going to get us into trouble," Kelly warned her. "Let's see what's happening in the waiting room."

A cluster of pilots stood by the coffee maker, discussing the smoke bomb. Kelly joined Dina, who was talking to three men at the counter. "Where's Dad?" she asked in a worried undertone.

Dina's face was pale, and there were tense lines around her mouth. She waved toward the closed door of the office. "He's in there with J. L. and another policeman. They're probably deciding what to do."

"I know one thing he's going to do," exclaimed Kelly. "He's ordered some dead-bolt locks for the hangar. Too bad they weren't on before this happened." The men were looking at her with interest, and Kelly resisted an impulse to say that Dad was the only one who'd have keys.

One of the men, the thin, dark-haired one named Luis Carbonell, left the counter. Kelly watched him curiously as he walked toward the hangar. Did Mr. Carbonell really have a prison record, as Aunt Jessica had said?

When her father and two policemen came out of the office, Kelly stepped toward him, and he glanced up as if surprised to find her there. "Tell Jessica I won't be back for supper," he said. "You two had better plan on walking home."

"Okay, Dad." Kelly wished she could ask him what the police had said. But the men were already on their way into the hangar. She found Tommie at her elbow. "You heard him. I guess it's time to start back, since we have to walk," she said reluctantly.

When they reached the highway, the dark expanse of pine trees beyond the airport reminded Kelly about Mr. Taylor. His cabin must be somewhere in all that wilderness. Tomorrow she was going to find it.

Wondering whether she'd have far to go, she asked Tommie, "Do you know where there's a fire tower around here?"

"Yes, there's one just down the road, in the woods on the other side of the creek. Want to go see it some time?"

"I sure do," Kelly answered with a smile. "Maybe I'll find some clues for that buried treasure you were telling me about."

A grin lit up Tommie's small face. "Or you might meet the Jersey Devil, or a ghost from one of the ghost towns." She pulled a tennis ball out of her pocket and bounced it as they walked along.

"There really were towns out there, about a hundred years ago." Tommie's words jerked in time to her thudding ball. "They used to make iron and paper and stuff, but after a while all the little towns died out. The woods took over everything. You can still see some of the old walls, though."

"Sounds like you've done a lot of exploring," said Kelly. "Do you know anything about the birds around here?"

"Birds? There's lots of them in the Pines–and there's flowers and all kinds of animals too. Ask Eva; she knows a lot more than I do. Have you ever heard of the Pine Barrens tree frog?"

"No," admitted Kelly.

"They're almost extinct," Tommie told her importantly. "But I've seen a couple of 'em. They're pretty: bright green with a white belly and a purple stripe down the side."

As they turned in at Aunt Jessica's driveway, Kelly's eyes were drawn again to the white tower at the side of the house. It really did look like an interesting place to explore. Maybe there was some mysterious reason why Jessica York kept its door locked.

Later, when Kelly asked about it, the answer was disappointing. "Too hard to keep clean," Aunt Jessica told her. "I got tired of dusting those steps when no one ever used them. I don't think I even know where the key is anymore. Here, you can wash these carrots."

She handed the carrots to Kelly and dropped a blob of ground beef into a bowl. "There are all kinds of spiders up in that tower too; it's a dreadful place. I wish that man had never built it."

"What man?" Kelly asked quickly.

"The first one who owned this house. Apparently he had a dozen children and wanted some place where he could study in peace; so he built himself that tower." She began pulling small covered bowls out of the refrigerator.

Kelly forgot about the tower and watched in amazement as her aunt emptied the bowls one by one into the ground beef. "What's that going to be?" she asked, eyeing the remains of last night's tuna casserole.

"Meatloaf." Aunt Jessica began grating carrots into the mixture. "It's a good way to clean up leftovers–my own special recipe. Next I'll add an egg to hold it all together."

Kelly turned away so Aunt Jessica couldn't see the expression on her face. Dad was lucky to be eating out tonight, even if it was just a sandwich at the airport.

At supper time she ate the peculiar-tasting meatloaf in small, quickly-swallowed bites while she listened to her aunt discussing the smoke bomb.

"I told Bob there was something shady going on out at the airport," the woman said, sounding satisfied. "He'd better watch that Carbonell man."

"I knew it," Eva murmured.

"What?" asked Aunt Jessica.

Eva gave Kelly a meaningful glance. "Bad things happening," she said, and her face, with its frame of untidy brown hair, looked mysterious. Kelly pried a chunk of soggy broccoli from the meatloaf and pushed it around on her plate, wondering what Eva was talking about.

Her curiosity about Eva changed to exasperation later that evening when she returned to the bedroom and found a dark, wild-haired face nailed to the wall above her bed. The creature was only a carving, fashioned from a small brown tree stump that had been turned so that its roots bristled like spiky hair. But the pointed face with its cruel, snarling mouth was disturbing, and Kelly snatched it off the wall.

She dropped it on the bed where Eva sat. "Is this another one of your pets?"

Eva looked up from the moth she was studying with a magnifying glass and raised an eyebrow. "Don't you recognize him? See his horns? I thought Tommie would have told you about the Jersey Devil by now."

"Well, she did, sort of." Kelly flopped down on her bed, wishing she had a room of her own. "Is that what the Jersey Devil is supposed to look like? " she asked with a sigh.

"It all depends," Eva answered. "Most people think of him as a huge hairy monster with the head of a dog and wings of a bat. Sometimes he has a forked tail."

"Where'd he come from?"

"He's a legend that's been around ever since the seventeenth century. Supposed to be connected with a strange old woman named Mother Jane Leeds." Eva paused, then added, "There are lots of stories about him robbing graves and screaming in the Pines, but no one ever did catch him."

"You're full of stories about the Pine Barrens, just like Tommie," Kelly remarked.

Eva put down the magnifying glass and brushed the tangled hair back from her face. "Old stories usually have a germ of truth in them," she said seriously. "I know for a fact that there are fierce wild dogs out in the Pines. I've sometimes wondered if they're descendants of whatever creature the Jersey Devil might have been."

"Have you ever seen any?" persisted Kelly.

"Wild dogs? Yes," she said coolly. "Sometimes I go for walks at night in the woods, but they don't bother me. I'm careful to stay out of their way."

Her solemn tone gave Kelly an eerie feeling. She made herself get up and rearrange her dresser drawers. No more listening to Eva and Tommie and their wild tales–or she'd start believing all that stuff too.

Early the next morning, while sunrise was still smudging pink across the horizon, Kelly dressed quietly and slipped downstairs. If she could leave the house before Aunt Jessica got up, she'd have plenty of time to look for Mr. Taylor's cabin. She was glad to find her father hunched over a cup of coffee at the kitchen table. Now they could have breakfast together.

"Hi, Dad. Want me to fry you some eggs?" she offered.

He looked up, and she saw that his face was lined with weariness. "Sure. You couldn't do much worse than Jessica, anyway." He yawned. "Worked late last night."

"How's everything going?" she asked, hurrying with the eggs. "Did you find out who set the smoke bomb?"

He shook his head. "No leads. Nothing. At least we're putting on the new locks today. That should help." He lapsed into gloomy silence.

Kelly thought of a question to keep him talking. "I saw an unusual plane out there yesterday, down in the old barn. What kind is it?"

"That's called a Wren. It's a STOL modification of a Cessna 182," he said.

"What's STOL mean?"

"It stands for 'Short Take-Off and Landing.' The Wren needs only about 300 feet of runway instead of half a mile like other airplanes. It can even land without a runway."

He sipped at his coffee. "It's got some interesting features, like the drag plates on the wings. They're called 'Wren's teeth.' And did you notice the small pair of horizontal stabilizers mounted on the engine cowling?"

"Yes, I wondered about those." Kelly smiled to herself, remembering that Tommie had said they looked like a moustache.

Her father sank a fork into his eggs as soon as she served them. "Mmm, good. Is there any toast?"

"Coming right up," she said. She buttered it carefully and put it near his plate, then started making herself a peanut butter sandwich. Maybe now would be a good time to ask about Mom. She didn't know whether he'd even phoned her since they got here.

But he had already finished his eggs. He gulped down the rest of his coffee and left the table, still munching on a piece of toast. "Thanks," he said absentmindedly. The screen door banged behind him and he was gone.

"Well, so much for that idea," Kelly muttered.

The sight of Eva trailing into the kitchen warned her that it was getting late. Quickly she wrapped up her sandwich. "Eva, I'm going biking out near the fire tower, in case Aunt Jessica asks, okay?'' she said over her shoulder. As Eva nodded, Kelly grabbed an apple, picked up David's box, and hurried outside.

Five minutes later she was coasting downhill on the highway. First the airport, then the sandy road, she reminded herself. After she turned off the highway, there was no traffic except for a white van that soon passed her, its wheels crunching in the sand. She nibbled at her sandwich on the way, finally crossing a wide, slow-moving creek. Here the road narrowed, becoming two tracks filled with fine white sand that made pedaling difficult.

The forest leaned close to the road and soon surrounded her. The tall pine trees, whispering secrets in their shadows, made her feel like a noisy intruder. She breathed deeply of the spicy pine scent and tried to concentrate on her meeting with David's teacher. Of course she wasn't nervous. David had been one of Mr. Taylor's best students, and his teacher would probably be glad to talk about him.

When the road forked, she could see the orange tip of a fire tower rising above the trees to her right. That looked like a good place to visit sometime. Following the woman's instructions, she turned to the left, and soon caught sight of a dark, peaked roof among the pines.

She jumped off her bike and wheeled it along a faint path that angled toward the cabin. As she drew closer, she saw a back door and realized that she was approaching it from the rear. She left the path, pushing her bike through the ferny undergrowth, and circled around to the front of the cabin, where she found another path.

The cabin was so old that its shingles had weathered to sooty black, patched here and there with moss. It squatted gloomily under a huge oak tree, looking as secretive as the forest itself.

For a moment Kelly hung back, uncertain. Then, trying to look confident, she parked her bike on the path and marched up splintered wooden steps to the porch.

# Chapter Six
# The Tower Room

She knocked, and the clearing around the little cabin seemed to fill with silence. It was a watchful silence that made her feel as if someone's eyes were on her back.

She took a firmer hold on David's box and knocked again, pounding hard on the wooden door. A dusty front window stared at her as she stood waiting, and she peered into it, hoping for some sign that Mr. Taylor was at home.

A voice jerked her around. "Hey, kid, what do you think you're doing?"

It was a low voice, deadly quiet, but it carried clearly from where a man stood half-hidden in the trees. He wore the brown jacket and cap of an outdoorsman, and a camera dangled from one shoulder.

Kelly scrambled down from the porch, her heart thudding as the man crossed the clearing with quick strides. His eyes were hidden by sunglasses, but she could see the thin, angry line of his mouth. She clutched the white box to herself.

He halted a step away, inspecting her. At last he said coldly, "Don't you know that this is private property?"

She shook her head, fumbling for the right words to say. How could she explain anything to this man? Finally she thrust the box at him and stammered, "David–he sent this to you."

The man frowned and turned it over with long, pale fingers, looking as if he mistrusted her words.

She repeated, "It's from David–David Durant. Remember him–last year in school?"

Without waiting for an answer, she turned to her bike, leaped upon it, and rode away from the cabin as fast as she could.

The path she took led to a sandy road and she followed it blindly, her heart still hammering with surprise and disappointment. She had never imagined that Mr. Taylor would be like that.

As she rode, she tried to remember what it was about him that had frightened her. He looked quite ordinary–neither tall nor short; neither fat nor thin. His hair under the brown cap was sandy-colored. It wasn't the way he looked–it was something else–something hidden and threatening that she'd felt in the man.

When her breath began to come in gasps, she slowed her furious pedaling, reassured by the quiet stretch of road behind her. But what road was this, anyway? The road she had come on went behind the cabin. Although this one looked exactly the same, she'd found it in front of the cabin, and now it was going up a hill that she didn't recognize. It must be the wrong road.

She pedaled more slowly, wondering what to do. Should she turn back and hope that Mr. Taylor wouldn't see her ride past his cabin? Or should she keep going and take a chance on getting lost in the Pine Barrens?

Through the trees ahead, she caught sight of a bony orange structure. A fire tower. She struggled up the hill, bending low over her bike. Maybe this was the fire tower she'd seen down the right fork of the other road.

The ground at the base of the fire tower was littered with broken glass; so she carried her bike across the open space. Finding a road on the other side, she looked anxiously down it. Yes, there was a turn-off, and it looked familiar.

She sighed in relief, and, reluctant to leave so soon, felt for the apple in her pocket. It would be nice to sit under a tree and watch for some of the birds Dad had mentioned. But where to sit, with all this broken glass?

She peered through a thicket of tall bushes and saw that the woods beyond were clear of litter. After pushing her bike through the shrubs, she curled up on the sandy ground at the base of a pine tree. Slowly she ate her apple, savoring its sweet juice and watching the shifting patterns of sunlight and shadow on the carpet of gray lichen at her feet.

A tiny scuttling sound broke the silence. A chipmunk had leaped onto a fallen tree only a yard away. He threw her a startled glance and whisked out of sight into a clump of ferns.

She tossed her apple core in his direction and waited patiently. The apple was tinged with brown before a tiny black nose poked out cautiously from the ferns. The chipmunk crept up to the apple core, sniffed it, then darted back to his hideout.

Kelly laughed at him and stood up. "Don't you like apples? Tell me what to bring and I'll visit you again."

Reluctantly she dragged her bike out of the bushes. She'd like to watch for birds some more or climb the fire tower, but it was almost mid-morning and Aunt Jessica might be wondering about her.

During the long ride back, whenever Kelly thought about her encounter with Mr. Taylor, she wished that she hadn't acted like a scared little kid. He hadn't actually done anything to her, had he? What was she going to tell David when she wrote him?

As soon as she reached Aunt Jessica's house, she slipped quietly through the living room, hoping to avoid any more housework. But Aunt Jessica stepped out of the kitchen, stopping her with a sharp glance. "Where have you been?" she demanded.

"Out to the fire tower. Didn't Eva tell you?"

Aunt Jessica blinked, but did not retreat. "Listen, young lady, it's not Eva's job to tell me where you go. Next time, you'd better tell me yourself or I'll have to talk to your father about taking that bike away." She turned and pointed to the vacuum cleaner.

"Now I'd like you to do the rug. If one of the ladies dropped by and saw how you girls have tracked over it, why–"

Kelly switched on the vacuum cleaner quickly to drown out the high voice. Why hadn't Eva explained to Aunt Jessica where she was? Too despondent to even feel angry, she pushed the vacuum back and forth across the endless blue rug. Was she going to spend all summer listening to this woman and cleaning this house? She had to get away, at least for part of the day. There must be something that Aunt Jessica couldn't interfere with–a job, perhaps?

Kelly stopped to consider the idea, letting the vacuum cleaner growl at her feet. Yes, a job was just what she needed. Maybe Dad would let her work at the airport.

All during lunch she felt jittery, just thinking about it. After the meal she followed her father out to the car and asked him.

He looked at her for a long moment, and the lines on his face softened. His expression reminded her of the happy talks they used to have and the fun they'd shared–back in Missouri. Somehow she had always felt closer to him than to her mother. If only Dad would talk to her now. . . .

He gave her a smile that was a shadow of his old, carefree grin. "I suppose we could try it. There's always plenty of paperwork to do. Dina never seems to get to the filing, and you could answer the phone too."

"Great! Thanks, Dad." She wanted to throw her arms around him, but he ducked into the car, gave her a wave, and drove off.

As Kelly turned back to the porch, Tommie skipped past, dressed in a red-and-white baseball uniform. She was pounding her fist into a catcher's mitt, and her shoelaces flipped exuberantly with every step.

Behind her marched Aunt Jessica. "Tamara, tie those shoe laces." She glanced at Kelly. "I'm taking her to her ball game," she said. "I'd like you to dust the dining room while I'm gone."

"Yes, ma'am," answered Kelly remotely.

She wandered into the dining room, wishing she were upstairs with a good book, and began dusting the heavy mahogany chairs. She dusted as far as the locked door that led to the tower and stopped to wonder about it again.

If she had the key, she could find out for herself what was up there. Thoughtfully she swished at the dust on the old-fashioned buffet. That little chest down in the basement–it'd had all kinds of keys in it. Maybe one of them would work.

It took only a minute to run down into the basement and look in the chest. Sure enough, there were several old door keys. She chose two of them that looked likely: a tarnished brass key that was short and stubby, and a black one that was longer, with fancy curlicues on its handle. Back upstairs, she bent anxiously over the lock.

The short key didn't fit at all, but the long one clicked neatly into place, and she pulled the door open with a sense of triumph. Before her were narrow, wedge-shaped steps that twisted steeply upward, inviting her to explore. The steps led to a small room that seemed to be filled with books and cobwebs. It had the stuffy smell of an unused closet, and Kelly's first thought was to let in some fresh air.

The window looked out into a world of leafy green branches. She peered through the branches, admiring a distant white steeple that seemed to glisten against the blue sky. She could almost pretend she was a bird in its nest, up here so high in the trees.

A sound from below startled her. Aunt Jessica's car was turning into the drive. Why hadn't she stayed to watch the ball game?

Kelly stumbled down the steps in frantic haste, locked the door, and slipped the key into her pocket. She snatched up the dust cloth and was polishing at the carved grapes on one side of the buffet when Aunt Jessica walked in.

All afternoon she watched her aunt, hoping that she would go off again, but Tommie walked home from her ball game, and Aunt Jessica kept everyone busy washing windows. Kelly consoled herself by thinking about the job waiting for her at the airport. Maybe Dad would let her start tomorrow.

At supper time, Aunt Jessica issued instructions for each of them. "Eva, you and Tamara do the dishes. Kelly, when your father gets home, you may cook two hamburgers for him. I'm going to a meeting at church now, and I'd like you to help me carry this food over."

Handing Kelly a silver cake-keeper, she picked up a platter of cookies and led the way to a grove of pines behind the house. A sandy trail wound through the tall trees for a short distance, finally petering out in the grass at the edge of a long, narrow graveyard.

Aunt Jessica paused, looking thoughtful. "This is the oldest part of our cemetery." She waved at rounded tombstones that were edged with soft gray lichens. "Many of these graves are more than a hundred years old."

She started briskly past rusted iron railings that fenced the ancient plots. A few minutes later she paused again, this time beside a more modern gravestone. "I have a good friend buried here," she murmured. "Mildred worked hard for God; so I'm sure she's in heaven." She swung abruptly away and did not stop until they reached the church at the far end of the cemetery.

It was a graceful, old-fashioned white church, the kind Kelly remembered seeing on Christmas cards. Each corner of the bell tower ended in a small spire that pointed up to the soaring white steeple. Tilting her head back to gaze at it, Kelly recognized the steeple she had seen from the tower window.

Aunt Jessica led the way up broad stone steps into the dim foyer of the church. "Thank you, Kelly; set that cake on the table. You may look around before you go, but don't touch anything. I'll be home early."

She waited until Aunt Jessica had disappeared downstairs, then followed a wide staircase up to the church's balcony. She looked over the railing and paused.

It was the most beautiful sanctuary she had ever seen. The white walls below enclosed dark, glossy pews that were padded with crimson velvet. The same rich, red fabric cushioned the chairs on the platform and, fringed with gold tassels, draped the altar. Over it all poured the radiant light from stained glass windows.

She sank into a pew at the edge of the balcony and brooded over the scene below, feeling unaccountably empty. All of this beauty–what was it meant for? Maybe it was supposed to turn her mind toward God. She closed her eyes to its splendor. She hadn't thought much about Him lately.

Back in Missouri, things had been different. It was Nannette who had first told her about Jesus Christ; and a few months ago when Kelly had accepted Him as her Saviour, everything in her life had taken on a shimmer of joy. From Nannette–and from David–she'd started learning what it really meant to be a Christian.

All of that seemed far away today, like some kind of a dream. And now she was sitting here in this church. Maybe she should pray.

She opened her eyes and stared at the rosy light streaming through the windows. ''The Lord loves you so much, Kelly,'' Nannette used to say. But God had let Dad uproot her, and now she was stuck in this strange, unhappy place. How could He do that, if He really loved her?

She could find no words to say to Him.

Wanting only to escape, she ran downstairs and out into the fresh evening air. Slowly she walked back across the thin, sandy grass of the cemetery, reading the gravestones with melancholy interest.

As she turned from the cemetery into the woods, she caught sight of a short, billowing golden-red tree that was partly hidden by clumps of Queen Anne's lace. She stepped through the lacy white flowers for a closer look.

The little tree's lower branches swept down into the tall grass. She pulled one branch aside and crawled into a space beside the gnarled trunk. There's room enough here to sit and read, she thought with satisfaction. And I'll be invisible behind these branches. The next time Eva gets into one of her moods, I'll remember this spot.

Cheered by her discovery, she hurried back along the path to the house and joined Tommie in a game of catch. Finally she heard the slam of a car door and knew that her father had arrived.

He sat down to read the newspaper while she broiled his hamburgers, and she wondered whether they'd have a chance to talk tonight. When she served the meal, he looked up and asked, "How would you like to go to an air show with me on Saturday?"

"Sure! Where is it?"

"At the Bretton county airport, about an hour's drive from here. I want to see how they run things–it might help me when we have our own air show. It's coming up in a couple of weeks."

"Doesn't an air show take a lot of planning?" she asked in a happy rush of words. "How can you be ready in just a few weeks?"

"Most of the arrangements were made several months ago," he said, nodding in agreement. "I'm just working on the details."

Before they could discuss it further, Aunt Jessica walked in the back door, home from her meeting. Kelly's father greeted her and then turned again to Kelly. "By the way, I got an interesting phone call today. Apparently that Wren you saw in the barn is being used for an undercover job with some government agency. I guess they don't want anybody poking around down there."

Kelly wondered guiltily whether he was going to ask how she got into the locked barn, but Aunt Jessica remarked, "I've heard some strange things about that airport, how planes fly in and out of there in the middle of the night. And there's something else, too."

She paused dramatically before going on. "The man who used to be the airport manager left that job rather suddenly. A lot of people wonder why he just up and disappeared. I'd be careful if I were you."

Kelly gave her father a startled glance, but he answered calmly. "Now, Jessica, you know better than to listen to gossip. I talked to that man on the phone just the other day." He took a bite of his hamburger. "And it's reasonable that an undercover job would require night flights. Don't you worry about me."

The phone rang, interrupting Aunt Jessica's reply. She answered it, then looked at Kelly, her eyes curious. "It's for you."

## Chapter Seven

# Go Home!

Kelly took the phone, wondering at the expression on Aunt Jessica's face. "Hello?"

"How are you doing, Kelly? How's New Jersey?"

The minute she heard her mother's voice, Kelly's throat tightened so that she could hardly speak. She listened guardedly, not answering the cheerful questions that came one after another. Mother sounded as if she didn't miss them at all.

Finally her mother seemed to run out of words. "I've sent you a letter." Her voice sounded apologetic. "Maybe it will help you to understand."

Understand what?

Kelly glanced at her father. He was leaning forward, looking anxious. Hastily she said, "Here's Dad."

She fled to the small library so she wouldn't overhear their conversation, and crouched on the window seat. But her father's voice boomed through the house.

"Won't you think about it some more, Lynda? . . . No, of course I can't! . . . Is that all you have to say?" He slammed the receiver down.

Kelly tensed, hoping that he would come to her and explain, and dreading it at the same time. Instead, he stalked out of the house.

As she watched him go, she tried to reason with her fears. Lots of parents had arguments–and everything turned out all right in the end. Didn't it?

Her question hung in the air, unanswered, like a threatening cloud. To get away from it, she ran upstairs. For once she didn't want to be alone.

She settled down on her bed to read, imitating Eva, but before long, she became conscious that Eva's dark eyes were studying her. She put on a smile and tried to deflect that penetrating gaze. "Did Dad tell you about the air show on Saturday? Are you and Tommie going to come with us?"

"Yes, I'll come. Tommie has a ball game." Eva cocked her head. "Something's the matter, isn't it? Still thinking about David?"

Kelly couldn't hide her unhappiness. "Yes! I miss him so much–and Nannette too. I'd give anything to make Dad change his mind and go back. I hate this place."

"Maybe he will," Eva said calmly, returning to her book.

Eva's words echoed through Kelly's mind for the rest of the evening and finally lulled her to sleep. "Maybe he will. . . ." If only Dad would! Going back to Missouri would solve everything.

The next morning Kelly made sure she was ready in time to catch a ride to the airport with Dad. She was determined to ask him what had been decided last night on the phone. She had a right to know, she told herself angrily.

To her surprise, he acted as if nothing had happened; he talked about customers and airplanes all the way to the airport. Kelly studied him out of the corner of her eye. His face was etched with weariness, as if he had not slept all night, and his blue eyes were dull.

She couldn't help feeling sorry for him, and it was hard to stay angry. The questions that were bubbling inside her began to fade, like soda losing its fizz, but they left a bitter taste in her mouth.

After Kelly's father had unlocked the doors at the airport, he explained to Dina that Kelly would be helping with the paperwork.

"That's nice." Dina didn't sound as enthusiastic as Kelly had hoped, but she smiled and added, "Let me put on some coffee, then we'll get started–"

She broke off as Ron Carbonell rushed into the room. "Mr. Jonson! You'd better come here." He held the hangar door open and pointed at the red Stinson in the corner.

Across the wide fuselage of the airplane sprawled looping white letters: *GO HOME TO MO*.

"I hope that's not spray paint," exclaimed Dina.

Kelly's father was already striding up to the airplane. He rubbed a finger over the *G* of the word *GO* and muttered, "Spray-on snow."

"Will that damage the paint?" asked Kelly.

"It'd better not," he growled. "Wash it off right away, Ron." He stared at the hangar doors. "How could anyone have gotten in here last night? We just put those new locks on."

He fired a question at Ron. "Could this have been done yesterday afternoon?"

"No, sir; I worked on that plane myself yesterday. It looked fine when I left," Ron said.

Kelly glanced across to the other side of the airplane. Mr. Carbonell stood there, examining the fuselage too. His face was grave, as usual, and she couldn't tell what the expression in his dark eyes meant. Did he know anything about this?

They went back to the waiting room. While Dina started the coffee, Mr. Jonson checked the glove compartment of his car and returned, still muttering to himself.

A few minutes later the freckled young policeman ambled through the doorway. "Hi, Bob," he called. "Everything quiet around here for a change?"

Kelly's father scowled. "You won't believe this, J. L., but someone got past those new locks last night. I can't figure out where they got a key–the extra one is still in my car. Look at this."

He took the policeman out to the hangar, and Kelly wondered who could have found the extra key. After the smoke bomb the other day, she'd blurted out something about the new locks. Who had been there? A couple of pilots, yes; and Dina, and Mr. Carbonell. Mr. Carbonell!

"Kelly?" Dina's soft voice interrupted her thoughts. "We can start on those work orders now."

Kelly's mind fastened suspiciously on Mr. Carbonell while she sorted papers. Finally she asked Dina whether she knew anything about the man.

"Well, he's worked here for several years," Dina answered, "and he's a really good mechanic. In fact, we sort of expected the airport owner to give him the job of manager after the other man left."

"Do you think he minded not getting the job?"

"I don't know," Dina said slowly. "He doesn't talk to me very much."

A pilot called in over the radio, and Dina moved away to answer him. Kelly filed the rest of the invoices and thought about what Dina had said. If Mr. Carbonell resented Dad's being hired as airport manager, that could explain why he would try to convince them to go back to Missouri. Was his son, Ron, helping him?

She found herself wondering what the man might try next. If he succeeded in changing Dad's mind. . . . She jerked her thoughts back to the work at hand, ashamed of her sudden hope.

After lunch, when Aunt Jessica handed her a list of things to do, Kelly wished she'd stayed out at the airport for the afternoon too. The woman seemed to do spring cleaning all summer. Or else she was trying for the cleanest-house-on-the-block prize from her ladies' group.

Doggedly, Kelly worked her way through the chores, and after the last floor was polished, she asked whether they could make some popcorn for a snack.

"Oh, no; you'll get it all over the kitchen," said Aunt Jessica. "Wait, I know what you could do." She called up the stairs. "Eva, are you finished with that dusting?"

Eva's scowling face appeared at the top of the staircase. "What?"

"You girls have been inside all afternoon. Why don't you take Kelly for a walk in the woods? You could show her the fire tower."

"Sure." Eva spoke with an irritable edge to her voice. "But not right now. I've got something planned."

"Never mind," interrupted Kelly, remembering the chipmunk. "I just thought of someone I promised to visit. I won't be long." Before Aunt Jessica could object, she left the house and headed her bike down the driveway.

When she reached the fire tower, however, and finally coaxed the chipmunk out of his hiding place, she discovered that he wasn't interested in the broken crackers she'd brought. He whisked away behind the fallen tree and stayed stubbornly out of sight until she grew tired of waiting.

Slowly she biked back towards the highway. After she crossed the creek, she realized that she was glad to leave the shadowy forest behind. It reminded her of Mr. Taylor and how frightened she'd been yesterday. Besides, she felt uncomfortable with all those stiff-looking pines towering over her. They made her wish for the gently-rounded trees and soft green foliage of the Missouri woods.

As she whizzed down the highway past the airport, another biker joined her: Ron Carbonell.

"Hi, Ron," she called. Might as well be sociable. "Anything new from the police?"

He ignored her question, asking sternly, "Where've you been?"

"In the woods. Why?" she countered in surprise.

He shook his dark head at her as if she were five years old. "Don't you know better than to wander around in the Pines by yourself?"

She decided not to tell him she'd only been as far as the fire tower. "Why?" she demanded.

"It's easy to get lost, for one thing," he said. "And there's wild dogs in there, and poachers; maybe even quicksand in the swamps."

He turned off at a side street, and Kelly pedaled on, wondering why he always had to sound so grim.

Right after supper, she checked the shelves in the library room and found a book about chipmunks. Before she had read very far, Tommie poked her head around the edge of the book.

"You like chipmunks, huh?" the younger girl asked. "Did you find one when you went off into the woods today?"

"How did you know that?"

"I watched you, that's all. Does he eat out of your hand yet?"

"No, I guess he doesn't like crackers," said Kelly. "According to this book, I should have tried peanuts."

"I've got some peanuts," offered Tommie. "If you'll let me come too, you can feed them to your chipmunk. He'll love 'em."

Kelly had to laugh at her confidence. "I sure hope he does. But we'd have to go really early tomorrow morning because of the air show."

"Okay! I'll be ready before you are."

That evening Kelly started on the letter she'd been meaning to write to Nannette. It was easy to describe Aunt Jessica and her house; so she began with that, then added a few sentences about Tommie. Next she tried to tell Nannette about Eva–what little she knew about her–and the Den Eva had fixed up for herself.

After changing her mind twice, she finally decided to include a note for David. She felt shy about writing him directly. After all, he hadn't said he'd write her and he hadn't asked her to write him. But there was the box: she did have to tell him that she'd delivered it.

When she finished, she felt oddly dissatisfied, filled with a longing that she couldn't name. Maybe it was because thinking about Nannette always made her think about God, and right now she didn't want to be reminded of Him. Abruptly, she left the letter and went to open the window as wide as it would go.

Cool air whirled into the room, fanning her hot cheeks, and she realized that the wind had risen since this afternoon. While she watched the ragged gray clouds scudding across the sky, she concentrated on plans for the rest of the evening.

First she would decide what to wear to the air show tomorrow. Next she'd finish reading the chipmunk book. Then she'd tidy up her part of the room so Aunt Jessica wouldn't fuss. Perhaps by then she'd be tired enough to sleep.

The wind, knocking gently at Eva's moth mobile, woke her during the night. The sound snatched her from a nightmare of wandering among wild black trees and sat her upright in bed. She wrapped her arms around her knees, still breathing hard, and waited for the dream to fade.

Gradually she became aware that something was absent from the quiet room. She studied Eva's bed. The humped form under the blanket was still. Too still.

She crept across the room and patted at the pillows that Eva had shaped to look like a body in her bed. So it was true: Eva did go out by herself at night, just as she'd said. Kelly lay down again, wondering where Eva had gone and what she was doing.

She meant to stay awake and watch for Eva's return, but when she opened her eyes again, it was dawn. Tommie was whispering to her about the chipmunk, and Eva was back in bed, sound asleep.

She dressed as fast as she could and joined Tommie in the kitchen. They pocketed Tommie's peanuts, left a note for Aunt Jessica, and set off, bicycling quickly toward the woods.

The wind pushed them along under a dreary gray sky, still blowing hard. Kelly had worried about thunderstorms cancelling the air show, but streaks of blue in the eastern sky gave hope of good weather.

"I'll show you a shortcut to the fire tower," offered Tommie.

"You must come out here a lot."

"Oh, yes, Eva and I have been all over in these woods. Of course this is just one small part of the Pines, but we know where most of the trails go."

"Aren't you afraid of wild dogs?" Kelly asked, remembering Ron's warning. "Or poachers or quicksand?"

"Sure," said Tommie. "It's dumb not to be careful. But I can climb trees better than any dog. And I can hide from poachers; they're not very smart. What are you going to name your chipmunk?"

Kelly had been thinking about that. "How about Edwin, or maybe Eddie for short? That's the name of the man who wrote the chipmunk book."

Tommie nodded in approval. "Eddie." She giggled. "I wonder what that writer would say if he knew."

When they reached the fire tower, Kelly showed Tommie the chipmunk's hideout under the pine log. They dropped a peanut nearby and settled down to wait.

Kelly heard the familiar cooing of an unseen mourning dove and began watching the trees as well as the ground. She was rewarded by a glimpse of reddish-orange. "Look, a scarlet tanager," she whispered.

"Sh-sh. Here he comes."

The ferns behind the log trembled and a small striped shadow darted out. He snatched up the peanut and disappeared.

Tommie gave Kelly a triumphant glance and tossed out two more peanuts. The chipmunk reappeared, studied them nervously with bright black eyes, and circled back around the log in a series of short jumps. He rushed at the peanuts, stuffed them both into his mouth, and bounded away.

When they had fed him all of the nuts, Tommie sprang to her feet. "See you later, Eddie," she said, pushing through the thicket of bushes.

"Let's go this way," she called over her shoulder. She carried her bike across the clearing and was coasting down the hill before Kelly could stop her. That was the road that looped past Mr. Taylor's cabin.

Kelly sped after her, hoping that the teacher wasn't home, or at least that he wouldn't notice them. The small cabin was almost invisible, lost in the pine trees, but she felt better as soon as she had passed it.

When they reached the fork in the road, a man stepped out from the trees and waved them down. Kelly recognized his brown jacket with a sinking heart: Mr. Taylor. And he was carrying David's white box.

She braked carefully in the loose sand but did not jump off the bike. Her grip tightened on the handlebars as he crossed the road toward her. Sunglasses hid his eyes, and his pale face was impassive. Like a mask, she thought suddenly.

She waited for him to say something.

# Chapter Eight
# Making Plans

The man's lips stretched into a thin smile. "I must return this to you." He handed the white box to Kelly. "It seems that you have mistaken me for someone else."

"Oh, you're not Mr. Taylor?" she asked, feeling foolish and relieved at the same time.

"No, my name is Thurston Grant," he explained in his cold voice. "I did rent my cabin from a Frank Taylor; perhaps that is why you are confused."

Kelly felt him studying her from behind his sunglasses. It made her nervous, and she said the first thing that came into her head. "Are you a teacher or a scientist like Mr. Taylor?"

"Ah, yes." He hesitated for a barely noticeable instant, then added, "I am doing some research on the frogs out here in the Pines."

"Have you seen a Pine Barrens tree frog yet?" asked Tommie eagerly.

He raised pale eyebrows in a puzzled manner. "Pardon me?"

"You know, the little green ones that are almost extinct. Have you seen any?" Tommie repeated.

"Yes, of course. I heard one croak just the other night." He glanced at his watch and turned away. "Now I must get on with my work."

As soon as they had bicycled a safe distance down the road, Kelly said, "He's a strange kind of scientist."

"How come?"

"He didn't seem very enthusiastic about the–what did you call it?–the Pine Barrens tree frog."

"You never know," Tommie said reasonably. "Maybe he hasn't learned about the rare ones yet. He was wrong about hearing it croak, though. They only croak in the spring."

"That's weird," said Kelly. At least he'd been nice enough to bring the box back to her. Or had he done it just so she wouldn't come back later and bother him? She glanced down at the white box and swerved her bike to a halt. "Look, he opened it," she said indignantly. "I can see where he taped it up again."

Tommie gave the box a curious glance. "What's in it, anyway?'"

"I don't know for sure."

"Maybe you'd better check and see if he broke it or something. Here's my knife to cut the tape." With a flourish she pulled out a red pocket knife and selected a blade.

Kelly frowned. "I don't like doing this, but here goes." She slit the tape and lifted the cover of the box.

Tommie poked at four small plastic boxes that were wedged into the box. "Looks like bugs in there."

"Mr. Taylor got David started on an insect collection," Kelly explained. "Those are probably some special ones he wanted to show him." She closed the box and put it back in the carrier basket of her bike, wondering what to do with it now.

They waited for a white van to pass and then pedaled on down the gravel road. Soon they reached the highway, but now the wind blew into their faces, slowing their progress. As they neared the airport, Tommie called, "What's going on over there?

Is something else wrong?'' She waved toward two police cars parked near the hangar.

''Why don't we find out?'' Kelly turned off the highway, more worried than she wanted to admit.

The wind spiraled dust across the parking lot where they left their bikes, and its short, fierce gusts hurried them toward the ramp. A small group of men were gathered there, next to the gas tanks.

Beyond them, on the runway, Kelly saw the tall white letters of two words that had been written in chalk: *GO HOME.* The words were boxed in by several crudely-cut lengths of rope.

''Those look like tie-down ropes,'' Kelly whispered to Tommie. She glanced at the field where airplanes were kept tied down. Sure enough, Mr. Carbonell and two other men were pushing an airplane into the hangar.

Tommie pulled at her arm. ''Let's go inside.''

Between phone calls, Dina told them that someone had written the message on the runway last night and had cut the tie-down ropes for five airplanes. Kelly understood why Dina looked so upset. She explained to Tommie, ''A plane could flip right over in a strong wind like this. That's why they're pushing some of them into the hangar.''

''Who did it?'' asked Tommie.

''The police caught a man prowling around at the edge of the airport early this morning,'' said Dina. ''They found the makings of a smoke bomb in his Jeep too.''

''Do they think he's the one who set the smoke bomb in the radio shop?'' asked Tommie. ''Was he trying to set another one?''

Dina shook her blonde head. ''I don't know. They're talking to him in the office now.''

Kelly bought sodas from the machine and she and Tommie sat down in the brown vinyl chairs to wait. A few minutes later her father came out of his office. He was followed by two policemen and a thin, dark-faced man with a ragged black beard.

As the men walked toward the hangar, Tommie nudged Kelly, whispering, ''Hey, that guy's got a princess tattooed on his arm.'' Kelly eyed the tattoo curiously, trying not to stare.

Before long, her father returned alone, looking worried.

"Are we still going to the air show?" Kelly asked.

"Yes, I'll be finished in a few minutes," he said. "Luis can handle things here. You'd better go on home and make sure you're all ready."

Back in Eva's bedroom, Kelly slipped David's white box into a drawer for safe keeping and hurried to change her clothes. She and Eva were waiting on the porch, watching Tommie warm up for her Saturday ball game when Kelly's father drove up a short time later.

"Who's that in the car with him?" Eva asked in a low voice.

"Ron Carbonell. He works at the airport," Kelly answered. "Tommie said he plays on the basketball team at your school."

"Could be. I don't go to the games very much."

"Come on, girls," boomed Kelly's father from the car. "We'll stop somewhere for a bite to eat, and then we're off to the air show."

They hurried into the car. Dad sounded as if he were in a holiday mood, Kelly noted happily. Maybe he had decided to forget about his problems for this one day.

By the time they reached the Bretton airport, a brisk wind had scattered the clouds and was dancing through the banners and flags that hung everywhere. Sunshine threw a sparkle over the huge, grassy field with its dozens of airplanes and throngs of sightseers.

Kelly studied the airplanes with interest, thinking that she'd never seen so many together in one place. Some were shiny new planes decked out with the latest equipment, some were carefully restored warplanes, and several were home built. She especially liked a jaunty yellow Piper cub that had a rubber band painted along its side.

"Do you think they'll have the parachute jump when it's so windy?" she asked her father.

"Sure. They can correct for the wind," he answered. "It'll be starting soon. I'll show you where." On the way to the parachute jump, they examined an alcohol-powered plane and admired the sleek lines of a long white glider.

"There goes an ultralight," exclaimed Ron. Kelly tilted her head back to watch the tiny red and yellow plane. It had no cockpit and seemed to be all wings, like a brightly-colored mosquito.

After the parachute jumping was over, they visited the bluestriped refreshment tent and ordered hamburgers and French fries. While the short, plump man bustled about getting their order, Kelly heard an indignant squawk; it came from a birdcage in the the back of a pickup truck near the tent. She wandered over to look at the bird in it, and Eva followed her.

"That parrot looks like Blue-Boy," Kelly said. While she was telling Eva about the parrot she'd seen in Fairport, a woman got out of the truck. Kelly smiled at her. "We're admiring your parrot. Is he a Blue-fronted Amazon?"

"Yes," the woman said. "He's a smart one, too." She leaned over the cage. "What's the weather today, Mister?"

The parrot looked up at her and croaked, "Let's go fly! Sunshine all the way!"

"That's pretty good," exclaimed Ron, coming up behind them.

"We take him to all the air shows," the woman explained.

"Hey, kids–food's ready," called Kelly's father.

They sat down at a picnic table to eat, and Kelly's father asked, "Is that somebody's pet parrot?"

"Yes, isn't he beautiful?" Kelly said. "I guess they cost a lot," she added, remembering what the woman in Fairport had said.

"That kind is pretty common," Ron said, "Probably cost only a couple hundred dollars."

Kelly's father nodded. "Some of the exotic kinds of macaws cost a lot more, thousands of dollars, even."

"Really?" asked Kelly, dabbling a French fry in the ketchup on her plate. "Who'd pay all that money for a bird?"

"I've heard of it," Eva agreed. "Bird collectors are as crazy as any other kind. The harder it is to get a bird, the more they'll pay. We had some really pretty ones in Brazil."

Ron gave Eva an interested glance. "Tommie mentioned that you two used to live in Brazil. Do you miss it?"

"Yes," she answered softly. "I miss going to the rain forest, and I miss the beach–I was just learning to surf. And there are so many interesting kinds of people too: Indians from different tribes, and Portuguese, and other Europeans."

Kelly glanced up from her hamburger, surprised to hear Eva talking so much. Ron was having quite an effect on her. Eva's brown eyes were glowing and her face had lost its sullen expression.

While Kelly's father made a phone call, Ron bought ice cream cones for everyone. He sat down next to Eva, saying, "Tell me some more about Brazil."

"I guess I miss the mountains most of all," she said slowly. "They're beautiful around Rio. We used to take a cable car to the top of Sugarloaf Mountain and watch the sun set. And you can see all the lights of the city and the harbor from there. "

"Sounds great," he said. "Do you think you'll ever go back?"

Eva's face darkened. "I don't know. Mrs. York thinks it's her duty to take care of us, no matter how much trouble we cause. That's how she's earning herself a spot in heaven." Her mouth twisted in a bitter smile. "I keep trying to convince her that she ought to ship us back to our friends in Brazil. Maybe one of these days I'll succeed."

"Come on, kids." Kelly's father had returned. "Let's go see the Bomb Drop."

They followed him through the crowd to a place near one of the runways. "Over there on the grass is a big white sheet with a black square in the center," he explained. "Each pilot is supposed to fly low enough to let his co-pilot drop the 'bomb' as accurately as possible."

"What's the bomb?" asked Kelly.

"It's just a brown paper bag filled with flour and taped shut. You'll see how it works."

They watched as plane after plane passed over the sheet and let their bombs fly. Flour puffed into the air after each drop, and then two men ran out and measured how close the bomb had come to the black square.

"They'll start the Spot Landing contest next," said Kelly's father. "The pilots will try to land as close as possible to the white mark on the runway."

The white line reminded Kelly of the incident this morning at the airport. "Dad, did you notice that tattoo on the man they took into your office?"

"Yes, I've never seen one like that before," he said. "By the way, the police think he's the man who set the smoke bomb. They also suspect that he's connected with a robbery from a couple of years ago, but they don't have enough evidence yet."

"What tattoo?" asked Ron abruptly.

"I guess you didn't see the guy," Kelly said. "His tattoo looked like a beautiful woman in a long dress. Tommie thought it was a princess, but she was holding a cross, and there were stars all around her head."

"Marielito!" Ron spat out the word.

"What did you say?" asked Kelly.

"Never mind," he muttered. "Let's watch the airplanes."

Kelly turned back to the runway, but she no longer felt part of the carefree crowd and the sunny, wind-blown day. She couldn't keep her mind off the tattooed man. He didn't fit in with her theory that Mr. Carbonell might be responsible for the airport incidents. And what was the matter with Ron?

She was still puzzling over his remark when Eva began talking to Ron about the Pine Barrens.

As Kelly listened, she could tell that both of them had spent a lot of time in the woods. Soon she heard them discussing plans for a canoe trip, and before she knew it, everything was arranged for next Saturday–with her and Mr. Carbonell included.

At first she didn't especially like the idea of having that somber man along, but finally she decided that it would give her a chance to discover something more about him.

In the car on the way back, everyone agreed that they should have a Bomb Drop at their own small air show. Kelly's father told them that parachute jumpers and stunt planes had been arranged for, too. They all talked eagerly about ideas for the show, and Kelly realized that she was beginning to look forward to it.

She ran into the house, humming, and stopped short at the sight of the blue envelope on the dining room table.

"It's from your mother," Aunt Jessica said unnecessarily, handing the letter to her with a curious glance.

Kelly took it silently and ran upstairs to the bathroom, the only place where she could lock the door.

Her fingers shook as she opened the envelope. She had a feeling she knew what this was going to say. Quickly she scanned the two pages inside. They were full of explanations that didn't make sense and words of love that she couldn't believe. And there it was–the one terrible sentence she had dreaded: *Your father and I have decided to live apart for a while until we can work things out.*

She made herself read it again. That's what the phone call was about. That's what Dad had tried to keep so secret. Just as she'd thought: Mother never meant to come here, not ever.

Something sickening and cold–a sense of loss, of betrayal, uncoiled deep within her. It inched up to her heart, and there it turned to ice. She clenched her hands, willing herself not to care. If she didn't care, then it wouldn't hurt so much.

The letter quivered in her hand. She gave it a shake and tore it into tiny squares. She flushed it away. Why hadn't they at least been honest with her?

With one hand on the doorknob, ready to leave, she caught sight of herself in the mirror. Who was this white-faced girl with rumpled hair and wild eyes? She couldn't let anyone see her like this. She splashed water over her face, arranged a neutral expression on it, then combed her hair.

At the foot of the stairs, her father waited, looking troubled. "Kelly, I should have told you–I'm sorry–"

She folded her arms tightly in front of herself to keep from shivering. She didn't care. She would not care. She stared at him without blinking. "It doesn't matter. Not at all. Do what you want." Her voice sounded harsh and strange in her ears. She had never spoken to him like that before.

He stepped backwards as if she had struck him, and she turned away, hardening herself against the pain in his face.

Aunt Jessica bustled into the living room. "Supper's ready, everyone. Let's sit down."

Kelly went through the motions of eating the meal, although her face felt stiff, as if it were made of cardboard. She was careful not to look at her father, and she kept her mind blank. It was safer that way.

At last she could go upstairs. The mystery story she was reading would help her get through the next few hours.

While she tried to concentrate on her book, Eva spent the evening washing her hair and painting her nails with crimson polish. She wore an air of suppressed excitement that Kelly noticed in spite of her own unhappiness.

It was late when she finished her book and drowsily began getting ready for bed. Eva stood up, stretched, and whispered, "There's a full moon tonight."

Kelly stared at her. "So?"

"I'm going out. Want to come?"

"Where to?" Kelly asked.

"The Pines. It won't take long if we ride our bikes. There's a moth I'm trying to get."

Kelly was wide awake now. "In the middle of the night? Can't you get it tomorrow?" As soon as she spoke, she knew she was wrong. "Oh–it's a moth, you said. I guess they're hard to catch in the daytime."

"Yes, and it's this one special kind–a yucca moth," Eva said, as if that explained everything. She sat down beside Kelly on the bed.

Kelly looked at her doubtfully. "How can you find your way around out there in the dark?"

"Oh, that's no problem. You can take a flashlight if you want, but it's not very dark when the moon's up." Eva inspected her long red nails. "I've always liked the woods when the moon is full–in Brazil too.

She leaned close to Kelly. "The Pines are beautiful by moonlight," she said, "like another world. You'll see." Her eyes gleamed with mischief. "Besides, you heard Mrs. York tell me to show you around the woods, didn't you?"

As Kelly listened, the anger that she had smothered all evening erupted into recklessness. Sure, she probably shouldn't go. But what did that matter? Nothing mattered any more.

She shrugged. "Why not? When do we start?"

"Mrs. York goes to bed early," Eva said. "We can leave any time."

# Chapter Nine

# McCord's Critters

Moonlight transformed the sandy road into a ribbon of silver. It threw a silken white sheen over the tall ferns and bushes that stood nearby, leaving the forest in deep shadow. The silent trees looked black and forbidding.

"These roads were cut in colonial days, you know," Eva said in a cheerful undertone. "I like to think about the stage coaches and horses and bandits that used to ride along here."

The lilting call of a whippoorwill floated to them through the trees, and an echo trilled nearby.

"Hear them?" Eva exclaimed in a low voice. "Oh, look— there's one ahead of us." She flicked her flashlight on for an instant and a pair of eyes blazed red from the middle of the road. "We disturbed his dustbath," she remarked, as a small winged shape whirled into the shadows. "Those whippoorwills are all over tonight, probably filling up on moths. They'd better leave some for me."

Kelly gazed after the bird. Maybe at least she'd see some interesting birds tonight.

But as she pedaled through the sand, watching the moon-shadow of her bike slip alongside, she remembered Ron's warning about the Pines. The whippoorwills seemed to be following them, and she listened uneasily to their soft, foreboding cries.

After a while, the narrow road swung past a section of forest so strange that Kelly almost steered off the road, staring at it. Trees were there, yes, tall pines and other kinds, but they were just skeletons, black and leafless, their stunted limbs stretched out in mute appeal.

"What's this?" she asked.

"Forest fire," said Eva. "Happens a lot out here–just whips right over everything. The pines seem to live through it; they'll put out little green tufts of needles after a while. But the others die. It's surprising how fast the ferns and things start growing up again, though."

Kelly turned her eyes from the blackened trees and gave full attention to the road, which had dwindled to faint tracks in the sand.

She was beginning to wonder how far they had to go when Eva halted beside a clump of bushes. "This is where we hide the bikes. We'll go the rest of the way on foot." Kelly patted the small red flashlight she'd put in her pocket, just for reassurance, and Eva stepped off the road with an air of confidence.

It wasn't long before Kelly felt as if the dark forest had swallowed them. The narrow, twisting trail led deep into the pine woods, seeming to go on for miles. They must have been following a stream, for once in a while she could see a shimmer of water through the undergrowth. Sometimes the forest opened up into a long stretch of pine trees that were knee-deep in ferns. In other places, patches of sand caught the moonlight, and strange-looking lichens felt springy under her feet. Occasionally another trail wandered off, losing itself on the right side or the left, but Eva marched straight ahead into the tangled darkness.

When the path widened enough for them to walk side by side, Eva explained where they were going. "There's a bunch of ruined houses out here–you know–from when people went off and left them."

Kelly nodded. "Tommie thinks there's treasure buried some-where in the old foundations."

"Well, I doubt it," Eva said with sisterly disdain. "But I found some yucca plants out here that someone must have planted years ago; they'll grow where it's dry and sandy like this. For some reason they're blooming late this year–I've been waiting for them."

"Why come all the way out here for them?" asked Kelly. "Why not plant them in your garden?"

"Mrs. York doesn't go for gardens much; too dirty," Eva said. "And most people wouldn't appreciate me tramping around in their gardens after dark. It's easier this way."

Kelly was beginning to get the feeling that this search for a yucca moth might be just an excuse for one of Eva's midnight excursions, but she didn't say so. The soft evening breeze had freshened as they walked, and now it was tossing the trees above their heads. Eva stopped, as if to check which direction it was coming from. "Hope Old McCord kept his critters tied up to-night," she muttered. "It's all his fault that we had to come the long way around, anyway."

"What–?" began Kelly.

"Oh, there's this old man who's paranoid about kids. He's got about an acre full of junk cars and he thinks everyone's out to steal them. So he's trained two Dobermans to patrol his place. Sometimes they get a little too enthusiastic and patrol this whole section of the Pines."

Kelly didn't say anything. She took out her flashlight so that she'd have something to hold and tried to walk quietly on the shadowed path, hoping that Mr. McCord's dogs were indeed tied up tonight.

"This looks like it." Eva stopped at the edge of a large moonlit clearing. Kelly gazed at the rampant weeds grown tall among the scattered piles of rubble and wondered why she had ever wanted to come here. But Eva was already picking her way between the bricks to the center of the clearing. She stopped at a clump of plants with long pointed leaves that looked sharp and silvery in the moonlight. A cluster of white, bell-shaped flowers rose on a stiff stem from the center of each one.

"Here you are, my beauties," Eva exclaimed. "And you're blooming!" She bent over the waxy flowers. "Got your flashlight handy? Oh–see–there's one! That little white moth. And here's another." She scooped them up into a killing jar as she talked. "It's just amazing how this plant has to have this certain kind of moth to pollinate it. Nothing else will do. And then later on the caterpillars live on the yucca seeds–"

She stopped, then lifted her face to the wind. "Well, what do you know? Sounds like McCord's critters are out hunting tonight after all."

Kelly held her breath, listening. On the breeze came the sound of dogs barking. Then the sharp staccato sound changed to eager baying.

"They've picked up our scent. Guess I got what I came for." Eva tightened the lid on her jar. "We'd better go."

She started off at a fast trot with Kelly close behind. At the edge of the clearing, Kelly stumbled over a brick, picked herself up, and hurried on, brushing at her knees. But she hadn't been in the trees for long before she realized that she'd lost track of Eva. And she'd dropped her little flashlight. For a frantic instant she stopped, searching the shadows with eyes that hadn't yet adjusted to the dark woods.

The dogs were closer now; she could hear them whining in their eagerness. The sound of their barking filled her ears. She turned from the awful sound and ran. Blindly she lurched through the matted underbrush, not stopping for brambles or rotten logs or low-swinging branches; and always, as she ran, she listened to the dogs crashing through the bushes behind her and the barking that drew closer and closer. Somewhere, far away, a whistle sounded, but now she could almost feel the dogs' hot, panting breath, and she ran faster than ever.

She burst into a small clearing and staggered over vine-covered stones. At the far end stood a low-branched tree, and she headed for it, remembering vaguely that Tommie had said something about climbing trees. Without warning, she lost her balance and slid feet-first into a shallow pit.

Panting, she huddled there on prickly dried branches, aware only that the dogs had stopped barking. Tall grasses swayed and rustled in the breeze, making odd shadows all around. Were the dogs creeping silently across the clearing? No, she could hear them now, galloping off in another direction. She sagged back against the crumbling edge of the pit.

Now that she had time to think, she realized that her knee hurt. The pit seemed to be stacked with boxes of some kind; she must have hit her knee on one of them. She heard Eva's low call and pulled herself up out of the pit before answering.

"Where did you take off to?" whispered Eva fiercely. "I almost lost you."

"I couldn't see you anymore," Kelly faltered. "And the dogs were so close."

"Yes, they were having a good time," Eva said. "But then he called them back–did you hear the whistle? That means supper, and they always obey it."

"That's good," Kelly mumbled.

"Pretty exciting while it lasted, wasn't it?" Eva said. "They've never gotten that close before." She led the way out of the clearing and Kelly limped along beside her.

"What happened to your leg?" asked Eva.

"I slipped and fell into some sort of hole, but it wasn't very deep."

"Probably another one of those old cellars," Eva said absently.

They walked through the underbrush for a few minutes and soon came upon a well-traveled sandy path. "This is the best way to go home," Eva said, "and shorter, too, since we know that those dogs won't be back for a while."

The path skirted a large clearing that looked like a parking lot. Kelly peered through the trees at a tall monument that stood in the center, bathed in moonlight. She didn't ask about it, though, trying to concentrate on keeping up with Eva and listening for the dogs. Who knew what they might do when they finished eating?

It seemed like a long trip back, although Eva said they'd taken a short cut to get to the bikes, and even after she was safe in bed, Kelly seemed to hear the dogs barking. They returned to haunt her while she slept, appearing in her dreams as wild black shadows in a forest of pines.

She slid out of her nightmare to the sound of Aunt Jessica's voice. "Really, girls, you should have been up long ago. You're going to be late for church."

Reluctantly Kelly dragged herself out of bed. The room swam in circles around her, and a dull ache pounded through her head. "Oh," she groaned, leaning on the dresser, "I feel awful."

"I'm tired too," agreed Eva. "She can't make us go to church." She shuffled into the hall, and Kelly heard her telling Aunt Jessica that they were both too sick to go anywhere.

She returned with a smug look on her face. "There. Now we can sleep all morning if we want."

Kelly crawled back into bed. But she couldn't seem to enjoy the luxury of sleeping in. What's happening to me, she thought, sneaking out of the house at night and then lying to get out of going to church?

Finally she drifted off to sleep as the household grew quiet. She awoke with her headache gone and lounged against a stack of pillows, hungrily eating the rolls that Eva had brought up from the kitchen.

That afternoon when she felt well enough to get up, she found that she had the house to herself. Dad was working at the airport and Aunt Jessica had taken Tommie with her to visit someone. After inviting Kelly to come on down, Eva had disappeared into her Den. But Kelly had no intention of going anywhere with Eva for a while, and besides, she knew exactly what she wanted to do. The tower, with all of its secrets, was waiting for her.

She slipped the key out of its hiding place in her dresser and hurried to open the small white door. Hoping that Aunt Jessica would stay away all afternoon, she climbed the twisting staircase with eager steps.

Now that she had more time, she looked the tower room over carefully. Two walls were taken up by windows, the third held shelves of dusty books, and the fourth looked like a wide cupboard. In one corner of the room stood an old wooden rocking chair with an arm missing.

Curiously she pulled at the cupboard doors. They swung out to reveal a narrow bed folded against the wall. She wrinkled her nose at the musty smell of the faded blue mattress cover and left the bed open to air while she browsed through the books. They seemed to be mostly reference books and sermon collections. At one end of a bookshelf, she discovered the cracked arm of the rocking chair.

That could be fixed with some glue, she thought. Carefully she closed the tower door and ran down to hunt through the basement shelves. She found the glue and was on her way back through the kitchen before she realized that Aunt Jessica had returned.

"You look as if you're feeling better, Kelly," her aunt said in a no-nonsense voice. "I'll expect you to come to church with me tonight."

"Yes, ma'am." Kelly retreated to the bedroom with a scowl. She'd hardly started her exploration of the tower room. And why did Aunt Jessica have to be so pushy about going to church?

That evening during the church service, she occupied herself with studying the bright figures in the stained-glass windows. But even the lambs with their gentle faces could not keep her attention. Last night's experience had left her feeling guilty and restless, impatient with the solemn beauty that surrounded her.

The same feeling of unrest clung to her during the next few days. The prospect of her parents each going a different way was so terrible that she couldn't let herself think about it. And she didn't want to talk about it either; she avoided her father, speaking to him only when necessary. A cold place grew inside her, empty and aching.

Eva had become more and more withdrawn. Apart from a hated math course that she had to take in summer school, she spent all of her time in her Den. Even when Kelly and Tommie went to Carl's Pet Shop to admire the parrots, she wasn't interested enough to go with them. The only thing she would talk about was Saturday's canoe trip, and even that made her complain. "Too bad Ron has to have his father along," she remarked one time. "There's something about that man that I just can't stand."

But Kelly looked forward each day to going to the airport. Her work was demanding enough to keep her mind off anything else, and the time went quickly. The incidents there seemed to have made everyone jittery, including Dina. Although she was as friendly as ever, Kelly noticed that Dina's green eyes had lost their smile. They were watchful instead, like a cat's eyes.

While Kelly helped in the office, she watched too, studying anyone who looked suspicious. But the more she watched Mr. Carbonell, the more she began to wonder whether she'd been wrong about him.

After a few conversations with Ron, she learned that he could be agreeable in spite of his gruff manner. She told him about Eddie, and they went to visit the chipmunk several times so he could take pictures. The chipmunk began to get used to them and would often climb right up to Kelly's knee for a peanut. Once she stroked his sleek brown back for an instant.

On Thursday Nannette's letter arrived, sooner than she'd dared to hope. She seized it, wishing for a place to read it by herself, and then remembered the small golden-red tree she'd discovered by the cemetery.

It took only a few minutes to speed down the path and slip beneath the low branches. She settled herself next to the trunk and opened her letter expectantly. Nannette began by telling her all the news she'd been longing for, including details about David's job at the airport and his visits to her cottage. She said that she was praying for Kelly's parents; then she mentioned Eva.

"Your new friend sounds as if she's had a difficult life and doesn't quite know how to handle her problems. She's probably trying to prove her independence in any way that she can. She may be a very interesting person, but remember that she doesn't belong to the Lord–and you do.''

Nannette's black handwriting slanted firmly across the page. ''Tonight I read Psalm 1 and thought of you. I'm asking the Lord to keep you from being influenced by Eva. And I'm praying for her and Tommie too, poor things. The Lord has put you there for a reason–perhaps to show them His love.''

Slowly Kelly folded up the letter, wondering why she felt so empty inside. Nannette always had to talk about God's love, didn't she?

That night, she took a quick look at the verses in Psalm 1 that Nannette had mentioned.

*Blessed is the man that walketh not in the counsel of the ungodly, nor standeth in the way of sinners, nor sitteth in the seat of the scornful.*

*But his delight is in the law of the Lord; and in his law doth he meditate day and night.*

Did Nannette mean it as some kind of warning? Kelly tucked the letter into her Bible and slipped it into the drawer, out of sight. But she found that she could not forget Nannette's words as easily.

Early the next morning, Tommie persuaded her to go out and visit the chipmunk again. When they reached the fire tower, Tommie scrambled half-way to the top and called, ''Let's look at the view first. I love it up here.''

''Me too.'' Kelly ran up the clanging metal steps until she stood high above the billowing green tree tops. She gazed at the narrow white roads that meandered off in every direction and wondered which one she and Eva had taken the night they'd been out. No wonder it was so easy to get lost in the Pines.

Tommie stopped abruptly on her way back down. ''What's that?'' She pointed across the trees to a dark form huddled beside one of the roads.

Kelly joined her on the step. ''A body?''

"Come on!" exclaimed Tommie.

They grabbed their bikes and raced toward the still figure. "It's that man," Tommie whispered as they drew closer. "Thurston Grant."

He was lying in a crumpled heap, as if he'd fallen over sideways from a sitting position. Kelly knelt beside him, wondering what to do. Although he was unconscious, he seemed to be breathing all right.

On the road beside him lay the sunglasses he always wore, and as she studied him, she noticed some odd black markings on his closed eyelids. She reached for his sunglasses and he stirred. His eyes opened and stared up at her accusingly.

He pushed himself upright. "What're you doing here?" he demanded, snatching the glasses from her. His hands shook as he put them on.

"I–we–saw you and thought you might be hurt," she stammered.

"Just my arm," he said. "Sat down to rest for a minute. Where's my cap?"

Tommie picked up the brown cap from the sand and handed it to him. Noticing a shiny bald spot on the man's head, Kelly wondered whether he wore the cap to cover it up.

"Is your arm bleeding?" she asked. "Do you want us to call a doctor?"

"No, it's nothing," he insisted, struggling to his feet. He stood there, swaying, and added jerkily,"It's–stopped bleeding. No–need for a doctor."

"We'll help you get to your cabin," Tommie offered, eyeing his thin frame. "Here, lean on Kelly. I'm too short."

"Yes–cabin–" he muttered, and Kelly took his good arm.

Slowly they walked down the road. Tommie followed, pushing both bikes and chattering to him. "You look like a poacher got you. Those crazy guys'll shoot at anything that moves. One of them probably saw your brown jacket and thought he was getting himself a deer."

"That's it—poacher," the man mumbled in agreement.

By the time they reached his cabin, he seemed to be feeling stronger and had shrugged off Kelly's help. He paused beside his porch, breathing heavily. "I'll be all right now." He struggled up the steps, fumbled with the lock, and disappeared inside.

Kelly looked at Tommie and raised an eyebrow. "I guess that's that. Thanks a lot, huh?"

After they returned to the fire tower, Kelly suddenly remembered her job. "Oh, I promised Dina that I'd come in early this morning. Say 'hi' to Eddie for me. And tell Aunt Jessica I won't be there for lunch, okay?" She waved goodbye to Tommie and turned her bike toward the airport.

While she filed work orders, Kelly continued her scrutiny of each person who came into the waiting room. Whoever had caused all the trouble was bound to try again. She'd almost given up on the idea that it might be Mr. Carbonell. She had found him to be a quiet man who treated her with grave courtesy, and he certainly didn't act like a criminal, no matter what Aunt Jessica said. But it was hard to tell what he was thinking behind those dark eyes.

During the afternoon, J. L. stopped by, his freckled face stern. He had a private talk with Kelly's father behind the closed door of the office, but no one seemed to know why. When her father noticed that Kelly was there, he told her not to wait for him, that he'd be working late again.

She biked home with the familiar cold ache inside her. Dad seemed like a stranger now. Every once in a while she'd catch him looking at her with a question in his eyes, but she couldn't think of anything to say to him except horrible, bitter words that would just make everything worse.

The sight of a waiting letter cheered her up. From David! Eagerly she took it into the small library and ripped it open. It was a friendly, newsy letter, and it sounded as though he missed her. Mr. Taylor had sent him a post card from the Rockies, saying that he'd decided to do some traveling this summer. So David told her to keep the box for a while until Mr. Taylor got back.

He described what he'd caught lately for his insect collection and told her that he hoped she would enjoy exploring the Pine Barrens as much as he had. He wanted her to tell him about the birds she saw and anything else interesting that was going on.

She began a letter to him right away. "You asked about anything interesting," she wrote. "Well, there's plenty going on around here." She put down her pen with a sigh. There was too much going on around here. Why did life have to be so awful? If David were here, or if she were there, at least she'd have a friend and nothing would seem as bad.

All during supper she thought about David, wishing she were back in Missouri. The meal consisted of a leathery noodle casserole that Aunt Jessica claimed was her sons' favorite. Kelly tugged despondently at the rubbery mass. If Eva were in a better mood they could've had some fun later on, making jokes about this stuff. But Eva had been dreamy-eyed and silent all day. Lately she spent half her time staring at herself in the mirror, or polishing her nails, or brushing her hair.

Aunt Jessica was in a hurry to get off to a church meeting; so she left strict instructions for Tommie, who had spent all afternoon at the park. "Bath and bed," she said firmly. "And Kelly, you can clean up the dishes. You'd better wipe down the cabinet fronts, too."

After Kelly finished in the kitchen, she borrowed a flashlight from the chest of drawers in the basement and slipped up to the tower room with a new mystery story. She shut the curtains tightly and curled up on the small bed with her book, determined not to spend the evening moping.

She must have dozed off, for she was startled awake when the front door opened downstairs. The flashlight at her elbow had dwindled to a feeble glow. Nervously she switched it off and sat up.

## Chapter Ten
# Mr. Carbonell

Kelly could hear quick footsteps tapping back to the kitchen. Aunt Jessica. The front door opened again and Dad's voice rumbled in answer to a question from Aunt Jessica.

She crept to the window and reopened the curtains so they would look right from the outside. Pale moonlight guided her to the bottom of the stairway. Listening to the voices coming from the kitchen, she thought that Dad sounded discouraged. Kelly sat down on the wide end of a step to wait for a chance to slip back to her room unnoticed. The talking went on and on, and she wondered sleepily whether she'd have to sit here on the steps all night.

The phone rang, snapping her awake. It was for Dad, but he didn't say much. When he finally hung up she heard a sigh followed by a thump, as if he'd sat down on the sofa.

"Bad news?" inquired Aunt Jessica's high voice.

"Not really. That was the man I used to work for in Missouri. He wants me back. Last week his partner quit, and now he's offering to take me on as a full partner at the airport."

Kelly sat straight up. A job back in Missouri?

"That sounds like a good position," remarked Aunt Jessica.

Kelly's father sighed again. "It depends on how you look at it. The guy is a crook, and I'd have to do everything his way. Besides, the airport here in Harding is a dream come true. I've always wanted to manage an operation on my own, and now that I finally have the chance, I'm not going to give it up."

He dropped his voice and Kelly leaned forward to catch his last sentence. "My wife can't seem to understand that."

"What about her job?"

He groaned. "We've been over that again and again. She's a legal secretary, and a good one. She could get a job out here if she wanted to. But she won't even consider it. In the past few years, she's become a career woman. It almost seems like she doesn't want to be a wife and mother any longer. That's why I brought Kelly with me. I was hoping my little girl would like it here. She's got to have at least one parent."

Kelly hunched herself into a tight ball, suddenly conscious that she was cold and the sharp edge of the step was digging into her back. She didn't want to hear any more.

The sound of her father's voice changed, as if he had risen and moved away. "What did you say is the matter with your car? Let's go out and look at it."

As soon as she heard him open the front door, Kelly stood up. This was her chance. Aunt Jessica was saying, "It just makes a sort of click when I. . . ." Her voice faded.

Kelly darted out of her hiding place, locked the tower door, and ran upstairs to the darkness of the bedroom.

"Where've you been?" whispered Eva.

"Never mind," she answered, hoping Eva would leave her alone. She wanted to think about what she'd heard.

It wasn't a surprise to hear that her mother cared more for her job than for them. She'd already felt that. But the sound of longing in Dad's voice had startled her. She'd been so busy hoping he'd go back to Missouri that she hadn't realized how important this airport job was to him. She'd never thought of him as a person with a dream. And he'd said it was a dream he wanted to share with her.

In bed at last, she stretched out under the sheet and tried to relax. But she couldn't help thinking about that job offer from Missouri. Maybe there was still a chance that he'd take it, if this job didn't turn out to be what he'd hoped. That thought reminded her about the strange incidents at the airport. Somebody else wanted to destroy Dad's dream. Who? And—why?

For a long time she lay awake, staring at the gray square of the window, while questions circled wearily through her mind. Rain began to fall outside, and its soft, soothing patter finally put her to sleep.

The next morning, Kelly helped Eva bake chocolate cupcakes and pack a meal for the canoe trip. They'd be leaving in the afternoon, as soon as Mr. Carbonell and Ron had finished with an airplane.

Although getting ready was fun, Kelly had some misgivings about the trip itself. Eva didn't seem to like Mr. Carbonell, judging from the comments she'd made, and Kelly thought privately that things might be rather dull with him there. But Aunt Jessica would never have let them go without an adult along.

When Mr. Carbonell picked them up, the girls climbed into the back of the truck, joining Ron and two aluminum canoes. Kelly's father rode in the front with Mr. Carbonell.

The truck bounced over a gravel road that led into the Pines. On the way they passed a white van driven by a black-haired man who returned Mr. Carbonell's friendly wave. Kelly read the writing on the side of the van: S&S GARDEN CENTER.

"What's he doing out here in the Pine Barrens?" she wondered aloud.

"Sometimes florists come to the Pines for pine cones or grape vines and stuff to make wreaths," Ron explained. "They used to get moss here too, but I don't know if they do anymore." The road narrowed as it went deeper into the Pines, until tree branches clutched and scraped at the sides of the truck.

Finally they stopped and unloaded the canoes beside a sandy trail leading to the river. Kelly's father waved good-by and drove off. The plan was for him to leave the truck at their destination, which was a landing point not far from the airport. From there he could walk over to the airport, where he had parked his car.

Ron gazed after the departing truck. "I meant to ask him if he'd heard any more about the body the police found in the Pines yesterday."

"Body?" echoed Eva.

"I guess it was a man who got shot. J. L. was out at the airport yesterday asking Mr. Jonson about it."

Mr. Carbonell's quiet voice interposed. "The police were interested in the dead man's tattoo. Apparently it was similar to one on the man they questioned about the smoke bomb."

Ron's face darkened. He snatched up the paddles and marched down to the river. Kelly watched him thoughtfully. Something about a tattoo had upset Ron at the air show too.

"Why don't you help me with this canoe, Kelly?" said Mr. Carbonell calmly. "Eva can bring the lunch."

Somehow Eva managed it so that she and Ron shared the same canoe, which Kelly had suspected would happen, and she was left with Mr. Carbonell. He suggested that she sit in the front so he could steer, and she agreed readily.

When they pushed off, Eva and Ron were still standing on the shore, arguing good-naturedly about who was going to steer. Kelly could tell from Eva's giggling that she was in one of her good moods.

Kelly paddled steadily through brown-tinted water that was as dark as root beer. She watched black whirligig beetles making silvery, arrow-shaped ripples beside the canoe and remembered that David had once pointed them out to her. Her paddle drooped into the water. Oh, David, she thought, I wonder what you're doing today. I miss you so much! I wish we'd never left–

Mr. Carbonell's deep voice interrupted, "Is this river very different from the ones you have in Missouri?"

90

"I lived near the Missouri River," she said. "It's wide and swift and sort of muddy." She dipped a hand into the water and watched her fingers turn to gold. "This river isn't muddy, but why is the water so brown?"

"It's called cedar water," Mr. Carbonell explained. "It gets this dark color because tannins from the cedar trees mix with iron from the ground water."

They had turned a bend in the river, leaving Eva and Ron behind, and the peacefulness of the woods and water made Kelly feel strangely unsettled.

Mr. Carbonell must have heard her sigh. "It sounds as if you are homesick."

Kelly nodded, too shy to explain, but she tried to think of an answer. Maybe she could find out something useful about the airport if she got Mr. Carbonell talking.

"I guess all the strange things happening at the airport make me wish we could go back to Missouri," she remarked.

When Mr. Carbonell didn't say anything, she added, "I saw the tattoo on that man's arm. When I described it to Ron, he said, 'Mario– something.' Do you know what he meant?"

"He was referring to the Marielitos, I suppose."

"Who are they?"

"Once they were refugees from Cuba. Several years ago, the Communist government permitted thousands of Cubans to come to America. Because they sailed from Mariel Harbour, the refugees were called Marielitos." Mr. Carbonell frowned. "But a great number of those men were criminals, allowed to come straight from the prisons. And in this country they have continued to rob and to kill; so now the name, *Marielito,* refers to the criminals, rather than to the many Cubans who have become good citizens."

"What does the tattoo have to do with them?" asked Kelly.

"Most of the Marielitos wore tattoos in prison to show how tough they were or what gang they belonged to. One of their favorite tattoos is the image of St. Barbara; that's probably what you saw.''

Kelly turned toward him, forgetting to paddle. ''So that man and the one who was killed might have been Marielitos? Why does Ron hate them so much?''

''Something happened,'' Mr. Carbonell said. His face set into lines of sadness and he gazed out across the water. Finally he continued, ''There aren't any Marielitos around here, but once in a while they come down from New York. Three years ago a couple of them robbed a jewelry store downtown. There was a lot of shooting, and in the confusion some bystanders were wounded. Ron's sister, Elena, was killed by a stray bullet.''

The canoe drifted with the whispering stream, and Kelly thought about the sadness in Ron's eyes. Now she understood.

Mr. Carbonell dipped his paddle into the water and added, ''A couple of the men got away. The police think the dead man they found in the Pines might have been one of them. I haven't told Ron about that part.''

''Do you think the Marielitos are connected with what's happening at the airport?'' asked Kelly slowly.

Mr. Carbonell shrugged. ''It's hard to tell. They have an underworld network that's growing very powerful in New York. Perhaps they want this airport for some purpose.''

Kelly shivered. ''It's scary, just to think about it.''

To her surprise, Mr. Carbonell smiled. ''I used to be afraid all the time, until something happened that changed my life. I was put in prison–''

A shout interrupted him as the other canoe swept around the bend. Ron ducked a spray of water from Eva's paddle and called, ''Hey, Kelly! Why haven't you taught your friend better manners? She won't even paddle right.''

Eva giggled. ''If you'd let me steer, maybe we could get somewhere. Oh, look over there–yellow water lilies!''

Kelly watched an electric-blue dragonfly alight on the pointed cup of a water lily and wondered what Mr. Carbonell had been about to tell her.

They paddled on slowly, waiting for Eva and Ron, who had stopped beside a clump of tall blue flowers. Mr. Carbonell was watching Eva. "It is good to see her laughing for a change. She has had a hard time."

Kelly was curious about the look of compassion on his dark face. "I know her parents died in some kind of accident, but she never talks about it."

"Yes, they were teachers at a university in Brazil; both of them drowned the same day in a boating accident." He glanced at Kelly. "For the little one, Tommie, it has been difficult too, but more so for Eva. I think she misses her parents very much. She needs a friend."

A burst of merriment came from the other canoe. Eva was insisting that she had to pick one of the blue flowers. Ron was slinging handfuls of water at her. "You'd better sit down," he yelled. Kelly turned around in time to see the canoe tip over, dumping both of them into the water. They splashed to shore, laughing at each other, and righted the canoe.

"It's a good thing we kept the lunch in our canoe," remarked Mr. Carbonell. He stopped paddling and let the canoe drift again. "Would you like to swim too?"

"No thanks. This water is colder than I'm used to," she said. "You were telling me what happened to you."

"Oh, yes. Well, when I lived in Cuba I was put in prison because I spoke out against the Communists. I lived every day in terror. I was sure I'd never get out of that prison alive." He paused, and his dark eyes beamed. "Then one of the prisoners who was a Christian told me about the Lord Jesus Christ. I asked Him to be my Saviour, and He changed my life."

Kelly stared at him in amazement. "This happened while you were in prison?"

He nodded. "Jesus Christ not only forgave my sins, but He took away my fears because He promised He'd always be with me. When I gave my life to Him, He became my best friend."

Kelly saw the joy in his face and wished she could feel like he did. In a low voice she said, "I accepted Christ too, back in Missouri. But I haven't acted much like a Christian since then."

A weight of hopelessness fell across her and she added, "I'm not even so sure that He's my Saviour anymore. Aunt Jessica seems to think that we can't really know for sure; we just have to do our best and hope that someday our sins will be forgiven."

Mr. Carbonell leaned forward. "Kelly, the important thing is what God says about it. How you feel or what someone else thinks doesn't matter. God says something very clear about this in the Bible. It's I John 1:9–*If we confess our sins, he is faithful and just to forgive us our sins, and to cleanse us from all unrighteousness.*"

She tried to look away, but he held her eyes with his steady dark gaze. "That verse was written to Christians, so they would know what to do when they sinned. Do you know what 'confess' means?"

"Yes, I guess that's sort of . . . telling what you did wrong."

"Have you told Him about whatever is bothering you?"

She shook her head.

His next question puzzled her. "I wonder, have you had a chance to read your Bible very much since you got here?"

"No," she answered uncomfortably. Then she hurried to add, "But I did go to church with Aunt Jessica. It's a pretty church, but the service was dull, and I couldn't understand what the preacher was talking about."

Mr. Carbonell nodded, as if he understood. "If you're not reading your Bible, that's probably why you feel so far away from Him. You can't trust God if you don't know Him. In prison I learned that when I read the Bible and talked to Him, God gave me all the peace and strength I needed."

He glanced at the other canoe approaching them and spoke urgently. "Kelly, promise me that you'll get alone with the Lord Jesus and talk to Him about this."

"Okay," she agreed.

He gave her one of his rare smiles and then called over to Ron and Eva. "You two look like drowned rats. Are you ready to do some real canoeing now?"

Ron grinned. "I'm hungry. When do we eat?"

"Just a couple miles more. At the rate we're going, we should make it by midnight," his father said dryly.

Kelly had to laugh at the look on Ron's face. He groaned and started paddling hard. "Come on, team; let's go for it!"

She was hungry too by the time they reached the spot Mr. Carbonell had chosen. They beached their canoes and perched high on a sandy bluff to eat.

"Hey, my second favorite," exclaimed Ron, opening the packet of chocolate cupcakes.

Kelly and Eva exchanged pleased glances. "You'd never believe how hard we worked to make those," Kelly told him. "And then Aunt Jessica made us clean up the whole kitchen."

"They're sure good." Ron reached for another one and Mr. Carbonell nodded in agreement.

"What's your first favorite?" asked Eva, her cheeks turning pink.

"Cherry pie," Ron said promptly. "I was hoping you'd ask. Do you girls bake cherry pies too?"

"Not me, but Eva probably can," Kelly said, wishing for the hundredth time that her mother had taught her to bake.

Mr. Carbonell stood up slowly. "Well, the sun is beginning to go down; so we'd better get back to the canoes. It doesn't look as if we're going to set any records for speed on this trip."

Eva nudged Ron. "Now it's my turn to steer. We'll get there much faster."

He laughed at her, raising his hands in mock surrender. "Okay, okay; whatever you say!"

They did make better time after that, and Kelly was glad. The sun had already slipped below the crests of the pine trees, and forest shadows stretched toward her like long black fingers. She watched the swift, darting silhouettes of nighthawks, dark against the dimming sky, and tried not to think about Old McCord's dogs.

She was hoping that the trip was almost over when Mr. Carbonell stopped paddling and pointed ahead of them. "Look at this, Ron." A huge cedar tree had fallen across the river, and smaller trees and debris had piled up against it, forming a wide blockade. "Do you think the girls can portage around it? We've got cedar swamp on both sides."

"I doubt it. What about going back to the other fork?" asked Ron.

"It'll take longer, but we'd still end up pretty close to the airport. Let's try it," Mr. Carbonell decided.

They turned back to the left fork of the river and began paddling swiftly into the twilight. Mr. Carbonell glanced at the sky. "We're going to be getting back quite a bit later than we'd planned. I hope your father won't be worried."

"Not him. He hardly knows I'm around anymore." The bitter words were out before Kelly could stop them.

"He knows." Mr. Carbonell's voice was gentle. "He has many problems at the airport right now."

"Well, I wish he'd left me in Missouri," she said. "Then he could have his precious airport all to himself."

"It would have been easier for him," agreed Mr. Carbonell.

His answer silenced Kelly. She had to admit that having her around had probably made things harder for Dad. Half-ashamed, she remembered what he'd told Aunt Jessica last night about wanting to take care of her.

From the other canoe, Eva called, "Looks like this river runs on forever. I sure hope someone knows where we're going."

"It won't be long now." Mr. Carbonell spoke cheerfully, as if he had seen the worry on Kelly's face. She paddled harder, and soon they were lifting the canoes onto a sandy beach. She helped drag them into the bushes and then followed Mr. Carbonell down a faint path.

"Actually, we're not very far from the airport now," he said, "although we're approaching it from the back side. I think we'll stop in there and make a call from the pay phone near the hangar. I'll let your dad know what happened so that he can pick us up. We'll get the canoes later."

They tramped along in silence, watching a half-moon rise and listening to the whippoorwills call. "I like birds that sing at night," Kelly said to Ron.

"So do I. You'd like to hear the frogs in the spring too. Some of them have the funniest kind of a *quonk-quonk.*"

"The Pine Barrens tree frog?" guessed Kelly.

"Yes," answered Ron. "Those are the ones that are getting rare; it's a shame."

"Tommie was telling me how pretty they are." Kelly's thoughts wandered to the man named Thurston Grant, who had claimed to be studying frogs. It still seemed strange that he had lied about hearing them croak. She wondered idly about his wounded arm and then remembered the black marks she'd seen on his eyelids. Could they be some kind of tattoo?

"Mr. Carbonell," she said impulsively, "have you ever heard of men getting tattooed on their eyelids?"

"Why?" he asked.

"Well, maybe it's because we were talking about tattoos, but I just remembered that I saw a man who had black markings, like letters, on his eyelids. It looked weird."

Mr. Carbonell nodded, and his face was grim in the pale light. "Yes. In Cuba I have seen them do it in prison. What were the letters?"

"I think it was *t-e* on one eyelid and *v-i* on the other."

Ron muttered, "*Te vi.* That's Spanish." He glanced at his father. "Sounds like the guy's a Marielito, doesn't it?"

Mr. Carbonell shrugged. "Could be." To Kelly he explained, "Some of the prisoners belonged to cults that had strange tattoos as part of their initiation ceremonies. They thought that a tattoo like the one you described gave them special powers."

He turned down a weedy driveway. "Let's go this way."

The road led to a deserted farmhouse that Kelly recognized as the one she and Tommie had explored. From here she could see the runway, outlined by dotted white lights as it stretched toward the hangars at the other end.

Eva stopped abruptly. "Listen."

Kelly heard it too: the rising whine of a motorcycle.

All at once she saw its headlight, like a single glaring eye, charging down the runway toward them.

## Chapter Eleven
# The Wren Flies

The motorcycle swerved onto the grass and lurched to a stop in front of the old barn. The driver jumped off, unlocked the barn doors, and swung them open.

"What's going on?" whispered Eva.

"Looks like a night flight for the Wren," Ron whispered back. "I've heard that this guy does undercover work for some government organization."

They waited behind the hydrangea bushes while the man used a short tow bar to pull the airplane out of the barn. On his way back, he ducked under the plane's wing, but his cap must have caught on something, for it fell to the ground. He picked it up, muttering, and Kelly saw the gleam of a bald spot on top of his head.

She drew a surprised breath and leaned forward to study him. His face was in shadow, but from the way he moved, she felt sure it was Thurston Grant.

After locking the motorcycle inside the barn, he climbed into the plane and started its engine. Landing lights flicked on and swung in a wide white arc as the plane turned, bumping across the grass. It taxied for only a short distance before rising smoothly into the night sky.

Kelly watched the silvery sheen of moonlight on the plane's wings and wondered about its pilot. So the government official Dad had told her about was Thurston Grant, and here he was, going off to hunt for poachers. That would explain his wounded arm the other day. Was it also the reason he'd pretended to be a scientist?

Still undecided, she followed Eva and Ron to the airport and waited while Mr. Carbonell made his phone call.

It wasn't long before Kelly's father picked them up and took them home. Eva, declaring that she was worn out, was in bed and asleep before ten minutes passed. Kelly undressed slowly, glad for the quietness of the room.

She was tired too, but her mind returned to the canoe trip, reeling off one picture after another. The dark woods. The gleaming river. Ron and Eva in their canoe. Mr. Carbonell. What a surprise he'd turned out to be. It seemed silly, now, that she'd thought he was some kind of criminal, just because he looked so dark and serious. And what about the promise she'd made him? She couldn't forget that.

She turned off the light and knelt by her bed. But soon as she tried to think about God, her mind went blank. A haze of darkness seemed to surround her, pressing down until all she could feel was despair. In a panic she tried to remember the Bible verse Mr. Carbonell had quoted to her. Nothing came.

She clenched her hands and concentrated on picturing the quiet river and the canoe with Mr. Carbonell in it. Okay, now: there she was, turning toward him, and he had that shining look on his face, and he was telling her that the Bible said, *If we confess our sins, he is faithful and just to forgive. . . .* That was it!

Quickly she prayed, "Dear Lord, You promised, and I'm confessing right now—I've done lots of wrong things since I came here. I've been mad at You, and I've ignored You and gone my own way; but I want to be different now, and You promised—You promised—please forgive me."

She waited, wondering whether the darkness would return. But it did not. Instead, she felt an assurance that He had heard, and with the assurance came a comforting warmth that settled inside her. Now she could sleep.

Kelly's first drowsy thought the next morning was a memory of happiness . . . something last night? Then she remembered: Jesus Christ. She still belonged to Him, after all. And He had forgiven her.

She ignored the distant ringing of a telephone and snuggled into her pillow to think about Him. Her Saviour–yes. And her Friend too, as Mr. Carbonell had said. For sure, she needed a friend right now. She was all alone here, except for Dad, and he–well, he was alone too. The thought surprised her, and she wondered whether he ever felt lonely.

Before Kelly could think about it any more, Tommie's pounding feet on the stairs shattered the Sunday morning quiet. She burst into the room. "Guess what happened?"

Eva groaned. "Go away, kid."

Tommie bounced onto the foot of Kelly's bed. "No, really, it's important. Mrs. York just got a phone call about her son Harold in California and he had a car accident and she has to go take care of him."

Kelly blinked at her. "She's going to California?"

Tommie grinned. "That's right. She's getting packed right now and your dad's going to fly her to New York to catch a plane."

Eva rolled over in bed. "Was it a bad crash?"

"I guess the steering wheel smashed into his chest, so he has a lot of broken bones but they said he's not going to die." Tommie jumped up and whirled out of the room, adding over her shoulder, "You two are supposed to get up and get going. That's orders from Mrs. York."

Quickly Kelly pulled on some clothes, saying to Eva, "Aunt Jessica must be really upset. I don't know who to feel sorrier for–her or her son."

"Well, don't feel sorry for us," Eva said. "Can you imagine what it's going to be like around here without her?"

Kelly stopped to think about it, and Eva imitated Aunt Jessica's high voice, "Terribly, terribly dirty, young lady!" She shook her head in mock disgust and collapsed onto the bed in giggles.

Downstairs, Kelly found her father already eating breakfast. As soon as he finished, he took Kelly aside into the small library. His lined face looked especially stern. "Kelly, I don't want you to go anywhere alone, even on your bike," he commanded. "And before you go out after dark or into the woods with anyone, you ask me first."

She stared at him. "You mean while you're gone?"

"No," he said fiercely. "I mean always, from now on. Do you understand? Not anywhere alone. Not into the woods."

She backed away, startled by his harshness. "Okay, sure, if that's what you want."

The severity of his face relaxed, as if he'd been expecting an argument. "Good girl. I'll see you later, maybe for supper." He turned to leave, then swung back and gave her a crushing hug. "Just be careful," he muttered.

Aunt Jessica, her nose frosted with old-fashioned white powder, was waiting for them. She reminded Kelly of several chores that needed to be done, and then, as she hurried out the door, added, "You'd better not forget to do a load of laundry tomorrow, or your father won't have any clean work clothes."

"I'll remember," Kelly called from the porch, smiling. Keeping house for Dad would be fun, and Tommie could help too. Her smile faded. She didn't know what to expect from Eva.

While they ate breakfast, Eva made it clear that she wasn't going to church that morning; so Tommie and Kelly dressed quickly and set off together on foot.

During the service, Kelly tried her best to listen, but the preacher didn't seem to be talking about Jesus Christ, and he used a lot of long words. This church was certainly different from the one she used to go to with Nannette. She smothered a yawn, pretending not to notice Tommie's fidgeting, and flipped through her Bible. In the back she found Nannette's letter and unfolded it to read again.

Nannette would be glad to hear that now things were right between her and the Lord Jesus, Kelly thought. While she was still reading the letter, the preacher finished, and then the congregation stood up for prayer. At last they could leave.

As they walked back through the cemetery, Tommie stopped beside a gravestone shaped like a tall cross. "What do you think happens to people when they die?" she asked.

"What do you think?" said Kelly, wondering exactly what to tell her.

Tommie touched the smooth gray stone, looking worried. "I just don't know. Eva won't even talk about it. She says it's bad luck to talk about dying. Aunt Jessica thinks that if you do enough good things, maybe you'll go to heaven."

Just in time, Kelly remembered something Mr. Carbonell had told her. "The important thing is what God says about it in the Bible."

"What does He say?"

"He says–wait a minute–I've got something here." Kelly opened her Bible to the front cover, where she had taped a piece of paper. She read to Tommie from it:"The Bible tells us that we've all done wrong things: Romans 3:23 says *All have sinned and come short of the glory of God.*" She glanced up and saw that Tommie was listening intently. "Nannette gave me this tract when I accepted Jesus as my Saviour. See, here's another verse: John 3:16. It tells how Jesus took the punishment for our sins so we could go to heaven."

While Tommie bent her curly head over the Bible, Kelly caught sight of Eva strolling through the trees toward them. "Here, you can take this with you," she said, hastily pulling the tape off the tract. "Read it, and then we can talk some more. Just don't lose it."

"Thanks." Tommie stuffed the tract into her pocket and waved to Eva. "Hey, what's for lunch?"

Eva's voice was mocking. "How could you be interested in something so lowly as food after your fine spiritual experience of the morning?"

"It actually was kind of dull," Kelly told her. "I don't know why Aunt Jessica keeps going to that church."

Eva threw her a curious glance. "What did you expect?"

Kelly gathered her courage and answered, "Well, I expected him to talk about Jesus Christ and the Bible so maybe I could get to know God better."

"Ah, we have a searcher for truth in our midst," Eva intoned dramatically. "Do you think you could pause for some grilled cheese sandwiches on your journey?"

Determined not to take offense, Kelly answered mildly, "Sounds good to me."

"Me too! Race you to the house," yelled Tommie.

After lunch, Tommie carried a stack of books over to the sofa and begged Kelly to come and look at the parrots. Ever since their trip to the pet shop last week, Tommie had been chattering about parrots. She'd even talked Aunt Jessica into driving her to the library and had brought home a whole armful of books describing different kinds of parrots.

"Look at this one," Tommie said, opening a large book filled with glossy pictures. She paged through the book, pointing out one bird after another, then stopped. "This is my favorite. Isn't he beautiful?"

"He sure is," Kelly agreed, admiring the bird's bright blue feathers. "What kind is he?"

"A Hyacinthine macaw." She rolled the name off her tongue with pride. "I've looked at all the pictures, and I've decided that this is the one I'm going to get. Those parrots in Carl's shop are nice, but I want a Hyacinthine. I'm going to save up my money." She patted her pocket, making the coins jingle. "Why don't we go down to Carl's and talk to him about ordering one?"

Kelly had picked up a smaller book with fine print and fewer pictures. "Let's see what this one says about your favorite." She found a page of description and read it. "I'm sorry," she said sympathetically, "but you're going to have to save up for a long time. This says that the Hyacinthine is rather valuable and usually sells for more than five thousand dollars. Besides,'' she added, ''it's Sunday, and the pet shop is probably closed.''

''Oh.'' Tommie gave the picture a regretful glance, then closed the book. ''Hey, I know what we can do,'' she said suddenly. ''How about going to visit Eddie?''

''Okay,'' agreed Kelly. Anything to get Tommie off the subject of parrots. But as they started out the front door, she remembered her father's instructions. She sat down on the porch swing with a disappointed thump and explained it to Tommie. ''He said especially not to go into the woods.''

''How come?'' Tommie asked mournfully.

Kelly shrugged. ''I don't know. He's probably been listening to Aunt Jessica talk about how totally irresponsible I am. Why don't you go on without me? Tell Eddie I miss him.''

Tommie's face cleared. ''Okay. See you later.'' She ran down the steps to get her bike.

Kelly walked slowly back into the house. She found Eva in the kitchen chopping parsley.

''What're you making?''

''Parsley shampoo. A girl at school told me that it makes your hair shine,'' Eva said.

Kelly glanced at her to see if she was serious. It wasn't like Eva to care about shiny hair.

Eva must have felt her look, because she added defensively, ''I forgot about it until now, and Mrs. York never lets me do stuff in the kitchen.'' She picked up the chopping block and scraped parsley into a pot of water boiling on the stove.

Watching her, Kelly remembered that Eva had been doing a lot of hair-brushing lately. And she'd been trying out different lotions on her face too. It had to have something to do with Ron. She looked at the kitchen clock. ''How far away is New York?'' she asked suddenly.

''About a hundred miles.''

"Let's see, if Dad took our little Cessna, he'd already be there. I guess it would take a while to get Aunt Jessica's ticket and everything. But he should be home soon."

Eva gave her a dark look. "I wouldn't count on it," she said. "You never know what might happen. Airplanes are dangerous–he'd be safer if he'd driven there and back."

Kelly had heard comments like that before. "Some people think so, but Dad always says that flying is really safer than driving. And I read a magazine article about it that compared all kinds of statistics like miles traveled and number of passengers and so on."

"But when a plane goes down, everybody usually dies."

"Oh, no," Kelly said eagerly. "You can land a small plane in lots of places. Once we had engine trouble and Dad landed in a cornfield."

Eva looked surprised, and Kelly decided that this might be a good time to talk to her about the Lord. "Besides," she added, "the Lord will take care of Dad; I just know He will."

"C'mon, Kelly, grow up," Eva said. "My best friend was a Christian, and she was killed in a plane crash. So where was the Lord then? He sure wasn't taking care of her. You've got to look out for yourself." She leaned over the pot and stirred the mixture vigorously.

Kelly picked up a sprig of parsley and examined it, trying to think of what to say. "I don't know about that," she said finally. "Maybe I'll ask Mr. Carbonell. But I do know that God loves me–Jesus Christ died for me. And He's got all the power in the world too. Maybe sometimes His idea of what's best is different from what we think." She dropped the parsley back onto the counter. "I'm not sure."

Eva didn't even look up. "Yeah? Well, what if something happens to your dad? You just might change your mind about that wonderful loving God of yours." She picked up the pot from the stove and headed out of the room. "I'm going to let this stuff cool and see how it works."

Kelly didn't even try to follow her. Mechanically she wiped up the remnants of parsley from the counter. She glanced out the window. The sky was clear. Why wasn't Dad back yet?

Finished in the kitchen, she climbed the stairs to her tower room, and as she stepped through the doorway, she felt as if she had come to a place of refuge. She crossed to the window and opened it wide, leaning out into the softly stirring green depths of the tree.

"Thank you, Lord, for this beautiful world You've made," she whispered. "Thank you for being here to talk to." She leaned on the window sill and rested her head in her hands. "Lord Jesus," she prayed, "I'm so afraid for Dad. Shouldn't he be back by now? Help me to trust You—no matter what Eva says."

Once she started praying, all the things that she'd been worrying about came rushing into her mind. "I feel so bad about Mom and Dad. You're probably the only one who can get them back together again." She stopped for a moment, wishing that her parents were Christians, like Nannette and Mr. Carbonell. "Do You want us to go back to Missouri?" she added hopefully. "And then there's the airport—it's scary, the things that're going on out there. Please show us what to do about it."

As her fears retreated, she began to think more clearly about the airport situation. If only she could find some reason for the things that had happened! And what did the Marielitos have to do with it all?

Ron knew a lot about the Marielitos, and he was worried about them too. Maybe tomorrow she'd ask him to help her to figure things out. He wouldn't mind, if only for his sister's sake. And she would keep her eyes open and wait for the Lord to show her what to do.

A breeze stirred the branches in front of her, bringing a whiff of pine scent from the trees beyond. Her mind turned to Tommie, out in the Pines visiting the chipmunk. She'll be getting back soon, Kelly thought. I wonder if she's read that tract yet. She found herself praying again, asking the Lord to help Tommie to understand it.

For supper that night they ate pepperoni pizza that Kelly had found in the freezer, and Tommie kept things lively by describing the antics of Eddie the chipmunk. After helping herself to a big bowl of chocolate ice cream, Tommie remarked, "Oh, I saw that Thurston Grant in the Pines today. He was walking down the road with his camera."

"Did he say anything?" asked Kelly.

"Not much; he wondered where you were." She grinned. "I started asking him about the frogs he's studying, and he stopped talking all of a sudden."

Tommie's words reminded Kelly of her suspicions about the man, and although she had planned to read while she waited for her father, she kept thinking about Thurston Grant. Why did she distrust him? What was he really doing on those night flights? Maybe he was smuggling drugs or something. Uneasily she dismissed her thoughts. The man had made a bad impression on her at first, so she didn't like him very well, that was all. Look how wrong she'd been about Mr. Carbonell.

She put her book down with a sigh and paced across the room to the window. Why hadn't Dad come home yet? It was getting late, and New York wasn't that far away.

# Chapter Twelve

# The Treasure Hunt

While Kelly waited at the tower window, listening for her father's car, she saw a dark figure slip across the shadowy lawn and vanish into the trees beyond. It happened so suddenly that she had to ask herself whether she'd really seen anything. As she stood there, peering into the dusk, she heard the front door open, then her father's voice. "Kelly, are you here?"

"Yes! Yes!" She ran downstairs.

He held her close and she clung to him gladly, sensing that the coldness between them was gone. "I thought you'd never get back," she murmured against the prickle of his unshaven face.

He looked contrite. "We ran into some delays in New York; then I got busy at the airport and forgot to phone you."

"What happened?"

"Nothing at all, for once." He patted her arm awkwardly. "I was just working on some plans for the air show."

She lingered while he poured himself a glass of iced tea. Should she try talking to him about the Marielitos? He sat down wearily and reached for the newspaper. No, she decided. He had enough on his mind already.

The next morning, everyone seemed lighthearted except Eva, who glowered as she went off to her summer school class. Tommie helped to tidy the house, and when they were finished, Kelly took her up to the tower.

"I'd love to have this room for my own," she confided.

"Your aunt can't stop you from using it–not 'til she gets back," Tommie observed in her practical way. "And she might not mind, if you clean it up."

Kelly asked her father about it when he got home, late that evening. "Sounds fine to me," he said slowly. "Jessica phoned this morning and said she'll be taking care of her son for a few weeks. Now I'm wondering what to do about you girls, all alone in this big house."

"We'll manage fine, you'll see," Kelly assured him. Because of the worried look on his face, she changed the subject. "Did Mr. Carbonell tell you we saw the Wren fly out on Saturday night?"

"Yes, he did. In fact, I've been curious myself about what's going on with that plane. Someone sent me a rather unfriendly note." He frowned, running a hand through his thick brown hair. "I was beginning to wonder if Mr. Thurston Grant might be running drugs on those night flights."

"Maybe that's it," agreed Kelly.

He shook his head. "Nope. The plane was gone all day Sunday. I stayed late tonight to watch it come back. I didn't want to interfere, but after the pilot left on his motorcycle I even checked the airplane. It was clean."

"Did you look for secret panels and hidden compartments? Maybe inside the upholstery?"

He smiled tiredly. "Yes, all those places. I know how airplanes are made. I'd have found anything that was there."

"Could the pilot have taken it with him?" Kelly persisted.

"Possibly. It was pretty dark, but I don't think he carried anything away. I can't have him searched without some kind of evidence." Her father dismissed it with a wave of his hand. "Maybe he was just doing something on Sunday that was part of his job. Do you need any help moving into that new room of yours?''

Kelly jumped up. She had almost forgotten about the tower room. ''No, but I want to show it to you. It has one of those little cupboard beds.''

That night while she was going to sleep, Kelly heard the tapping of Eva's mobile and thought contentedly that this was the last time she'd have to listen to it. She was sure she'd sleep better in the tower room; at least there wouldn't be anybody coming and going in the middle of the night. What else did Eva do besides catch moths on her moonlit trips? she wondered.

I hope she doesn't ask me to go again, Kelly thought, remembering how scared she'd been that night. But it's a good thing Eva found me in that old cellar hole, or I'd have been lost for sure. Sleepily she wondered about the boxes in the hole. Tommie was always talking about old ruins in the Pines; maybe she'd know what those boxes could be.

The next morning, Tommie agreed to help Kelly clean up the tower room. Energetically she vacuumed down the cobwebs, exclaiming, ''Run for your lives, spiders, here we come.''

Kelly had decided that the musty blue mattress cover had to be washed, and when she stripped it from the bed, an old-fashioned wooden embroidery hoop fell to the floor. Curiously she picked it up. It still held a piece of yellowed cloth with part of a motto embroidered on it in red yarn. The red letters staggered crookedly across the fabric, as if its owner had not been very good at embroidery.

''Psalm 28:7,'' she read. ''The Lord is—'' She gazed at the rusty needle, still threaded with snarled yarn. ''Somebody started this and never finished it. I wonder why?''

Tommie had switched off the vacuum cleaner, and now she gave the embroidery a scornful look. ''Somebody couldn't stand doing it any longer, that's why. Some kid like me.'' She made a face. ''Mrs. York tried to teach me that stuff and I hated it too.''

Kelly smiled and set the embroidery on a shelf, picturing the rebellious little girl who must have hidden her sewing under a mattress cover, years and years ago. It certainly was just like something that Tommie would do.

She returned to the bed, and while she finished making it, she remembered to ask Tommie about the boxes in the cellar hole.

Tommie's eyes sparkled. "I'll bet it's treasure. I told you there's treasure out in the Pines. Some robber meant to come back and get those boxes but he died instead. Let's go look at them."

"Wait a minute." Kelly had to laugh at Tommie's eagerness. "I don't even know where they are, except that the place is near a clearing with some kind of monument in it."

Tommie frowned. "A monument?"

"Made out of stone, I guess. It was tall and shaped like this." Kelly sketched an outline in the dust on the window sill.

Tommie nodded. "Oh, the Memorial. It's pretty far out, but I can take you there."

"When we go to the airport this afternoon, I'll ask Dad if it's all right," Kelly promised. "But don't go telling everybody we're looking for treasure."

At the airport she found a stack of work orders waiting to be filed. "I'm sure glad you're here to do these," Dina said. She yawned. "That was some flight yesterday."

"You fly on your day off too?" Kelly said with a laugh. "Where'd you go?"

"Oh, I had to deliver something for a friend." Today she wore her long blonde hair tied back into a ponytail that made her look like a pretty teen-ager, but her eyes were shadowed and remote. "And I meant to tell you, I won't be here this afternoon– I'm taking a student on his first cross-country flight."

"Don't forget your coffee," Kelly teased. It was a standing joke with all the pilots that Dina couldn't fly without her coffee.

Dina smiled. "Hey, that's right. Good thing I just made some fresh." She filled her stainless-steel thermos from the coffee pot. "I sure hope this guy doesn't dump us both in the ocean by mistake." She picked up the brown leather flight bag that held her charts. "See you later."

Kelly tapped on the open door of her father's office. When he looked up, she asked, "Can I go into the woods with Tommie this afternoon? She wants to show me something."

He was silent for a moment, drumming his fingers on the desk top, frowning. "Isn't there someone older who could go along too? Maybe Ron?"

"Sure, I'll ask him after work," agreed Kelly. It was almost time for Ron to get off, so she hurried through the rest of the work orders.

When she walked into the hangar to find Ron, Mr. Carbonell greeted her with his quiet smile. "You're looking happier today, Kelly. Why is that?"

"I guess you can tell." She smiled back at him. "I got things straightened out with the Lord. I feel a lot better now."

"Good. Now don't just coast along on that feeling. Remember to get some spiritual food."

She gave him a puzzled glance and he explained. "God gave us the Bible so we can learn about Him and grow spiritually. It's important for you to read it every day–just as important as eating. Once a week at church isn't enough."

She mumbled, "I went to church on Sunday, but they didn't say much about the Bible."

"Perhaps you can find a better church," he said kindly, "but don't wait for that. It's up to you to get to know the Lord Jesus for yourself. I've been reading in the Gospel of Mark lately. You might want to try it."

She watched him putting screwdrivers and wrenches into the drawers of his tall red tool chest. This man sounded just like Nannette. And David too, she remembered; David had said a lot this summer about reading his Bible. Was that why they were such strong Christians? "All right, I'll start tonight," she said firmly.

"Good for you." Mr. Carbonell gave her an encouraging nod as he locked his tool chest.

Ron walked over from the radio shop with Tommie following close behind. "Hey, Kelly, what's this I hear about buried treasure?"

"Tommie!" Kelly gave her an indignant look. "You weren't supposed to tell." To Ron she said, "I was wondering if you'd mind coming with us. My dad seems to think the woods aren't safe anymore."

He nodded. "Sure. I'm finished here. Lead on, Tommie."

The quiet clearing in the pines was larger than Kelly had remembered, and a road led into it from one end. In its center stood a tapering gray structure that reminded her of an elaborate tombstone. She left the woods to study it more closely, and the sound of coarse gravel crunching under her feet sounded loud in the sun-baked silence.

She shaded her eyes with one hand and looked up at it. "What's this for?"

"It's in memory of a famous Mexican flyer who crashed here on the way back from a good-will flight to New York," said Ron. "They say he ran into a thunderstorm."

"How sad," Kelly murmured, tracing the raised outline of a falling eagle on one side of the monument. She squinted through glaring sunlight at the inscription, written in both English and Spanish.

"Oh, aren't you hot?" exclaimed Tommie. "Let's get back into the woods." She sprinted across the gravel ahead of them.

Kelly paused when she reached the shade, gazing back dreamily at the monument that stood tall and desolate under the fiery sun.

"Now that's interesting," murmured Ron. He had gone ahead through the trees to a long, open strip of ground behind the Memorial parking lot. Now he bent closer to study the ground at his feet.

"What?" Tommie darted over to him.

He caught her arm. "Slow down. Don't step on it." He pointed to the straight lines imprinted in a soft damp spot near the edge of the clearing.

"Tire tracks?" asked Kelly.

"From an airplane. See, the lines are straight, without the patterned tread that car tires have." He walked back to the center

of the clearing. "Out here the ground is too rough to show tracks, probably. Yeah, here's another soft spot and more tracks."

"Aren't we going to look for the treasure?" asked Tommie, hopping from one foot to the other.

"Let's go," said Ron, but he glanced back over his shoulder as he followed her.

Kelly searched through the woods around the Memorial parking lot until she found a trail that looked like the one she and Eva had used when they passed by the Memorial. She paused.

"It wasn't very far from here," she said hesitantly, "but I'm not sure exactly which direction to go."

"How about we spread out a little–say twenty feet apart–and each go off at a different angle," suggested Ron. "Kelly, you walk straight ahead. I'll slant off this way, and Tommie can take the other side."

A few minutes later Tommie called, "Here's a clearing, but it's pretty small."

"Does it have a big tree at one end?" called Kelly, suddenly remembering.

"Nope. No big tree."

Not to be discouraged, Kelly pushed on through low bushes and ferns toward what seemed like an opening in the trees ahead of her. She saw a spot of red near a weedy pile of bricks. "My flashlight!" she exclaimed, picking it up. "I must be going the right way." A minute later she paused at the edge of a clearing. At the far end stood a low-branched maple tree, looking out of place in the forest of pines. "Over here," she cried happily, recognizing the tree.

The clearing had several piles of brick ruins, and she examined them while she waited for Tommie and Ron. By the time she found the remains of a cellar hole, Tommie and Ron were there to help her look.

"This one has the branches in it that I remembered," she said, pulling at a pile of prickly dried pine boughs.

"Huh! What happened to the boxes?" She stared at the stony bottom of the hole.

"Are you sure this is the place?" asked Ron. "Boxes don't just disappear by themselves."

"I'm pretty sure." Kelly heard the uncertainty in her voice, and she frowned up at the maple tree. "That looks like the tree I saw." She waved the flashlight. "And I found the flashlight I dropped."

"Maybe it's another cellar hole," Tommie suggested.

They scuffed farther back in the clearing and found the bricks of another ruin poking through the weeds like the bones of a forgotten skeleton, but except for a scuttling lizard, its cellar hole was empty too.

"I don't know, Kelly." Ron wiped the perspiration from his face. "Maybe you just dreamed this one night." He raised an eyebrow and added with a teasing grin, "Were you running away from something–the Jersey Devil, maybe?"

Kelly tried to smile back at him. "Not the Jersey Devil! But it was pretty scary." She wanted to tell Ron about the dogs, but she didn't really want to admit that she'd been out here in the middle of the night with Eva, even if the moth seemed like a reasonable excuse. Besides, Tommie was listening curiously, and telling Tommie something was like telling the whole world.

Ron glanced at her, his dark eyes serious now. "Hey, it's okay; don't look so frightened. I believe you."

Tommie grabbed at her hand. "I do too."

She felt the warmth of Tommie's thin little hand in her own and laughed unsteadily. "Thanks." Regretfully she added, "Looks like there's nothing here. Maybe we'd better give it up."

When they passed the Memorial parking lot on the way back, Ron fell silent, and Kelly guessed that he was thinking about the airplane tire tracks again.

"What would a plane be doing out here, anyway?" she wondered aloud.

"Taking on passengers or cargo–which is crazy out here in the wilderness."

"Maybe they're the ones who took my boxes," she said with a grin. But Ron didn't laugh; so she considered the idea seriously. "They could have had them stashed here for some reason."

Tommie interrupted, "That place doesn't have a runway like the airport. Wouldn't an airplane crash into the monument or something?"

"We came here the back way, along a path," Ron pointed out. "Remember, there's a road right next to the parking lot. There might be room for a plane to land if it had STOL capabilities. And there were some big open places back behind the Memorial."

Kelly stopped short. "The Wren!"

Ron gave her an approving glance. "You're right. The Wren would be perfect."

Tommie nodded, apparently satisfied, and skipped ahead of them.

"I have the weirdest feeling about that man who flies the Wren," Kelly told Ron in a low voice. "But there's no proof that he's doing anything illegal. Dad searched the plane after it came back and didn't find a thing."

"Who is he, anyway?"

"I guess his name is Thurston Grant—he's renting a cabin in the woods over by the fire tower. He told me that he's a scientist, but everyone at the airport thinks he's a government official doing undercover work."

"Maybe he is," Ron said slowly. "He could have landed at the Memorial to check on poachers."

"Yes," agreed Kelly. "But there's something fake about him. I can't forget that he lied to me about being a scientist. If he really were researching frogs, he'd know that the Pine Barrens tree frog doesn't croak in summer."

"He should," Ron said. "Maybe he's pretending to be a scientist so people won't know he's working for the government. He should have researched it better, though."

Kelly was too hot and tired to argue with him. She'd reached a dead end in the puzzle of Thurston Grant. It seemed that there was one more thing, though, one detail about the man that she meant to tell Ron. Whatever it was, she'd forgotten it.

They tramped to the place where they'd left their bikes, talking idly. The warm, pine-scented air clung heavily to them, and Kelly's shirt felt sticky on her back. The forest stood quiet, as if even the voices of birds and insects had been stifled. Kelly remembered that she'd wanted to ask Ron about the Marielitos. Not now, she decided. She'd wait until her mind wasn't so fuzzy.

It was a relief to get onto her bike and ride away from the trees. She felt better with cooler air rushing by, even though heat still glared up at her from the white road and there were several miles yet to go.

When they reached the house, Tommie grabbed up her bat and ball as if they were long-lost friends and headed for the park. "Come back by supper time," Kelly called after her, just as Aunt Jessica would have done. Suddenly she remembered what Aunt Jessica had said about the laundry. Dad wouldn't think much of her housekeeping if he didn't have any clean clothes to wear.

She ran down to the basement to do the wash, and as she turned on the washing machine, Eva came down the steps, carrying a fresh supply of leaves. "Lunch for your pets?" asked Kelly with a smile.

But Eva gave her a cold stare. "Did you have a nice walk in the Pines?"

"Well, it was awfully hot. But there were these boxes, and Tommie thought–" She broke off. "What's the matter?"

Eva's face was flushed and angry. "I suppose Ron just happened to be going that way?"

"Dad made me ask Ron to come with us," Kelly said indignantly. Now she knew what was bothering Eva. "Your imagination's working overtime," she said. That was an expression her mother always used on her, and it seemed to calm Eva, for the flush faded from her cheeks, and she shifted the branches in her arms as if she were embarrassed.

"Oh. Well. I just didn't know what to think." She handed a small plastic bag to Kelly. "Here's some bagworm cases. Want to carry them for me? I've got a box all ready so I can see what happens when the moths come out.''

Kelly felt more like handing the bag right back to her, but at least the girl was trying to make up for being rude. Maybe, like Mr. Carbonell said, she really did need a friend.

As Eva bent to open the sliding panel, she flipped her long hair out of the way, and Kelly noticed how clean and shiny it looked. That parsley shampoo certainly has worked, she thought. Or else it's all that brushing. I hope Ron appreciates it.

# Chapter Thirteen

# Puzzling It Out

Eva tumbled the bagworm cases out onto the table and Kelly glanced at them curiously. But they were just ugly brown cocoons with little tufts of cedar sticking to them. She picked one up, gingerly, and a plump black caterpillar poked his head out as though looking for something to eat. Quickly she dropped it into the box that Eva had prepared. "Did you get your yucca moths spread and pinned?" she asked.

"Yes, over there." Eva motioned to the spreading board at the other end of the table. "I'm going to go back and get some more while the flowers are still blooming. Want to go tonight?"

"No thanks," Kelly said firmly. "Not me. I still have nightmares about those dogs."

Eva's busy hands stopped for a minute. "I have nightmares too," she said. "Only they're usually about God. I always dream about Him being this big, terrifying sort of judge or something." She frowned and turned away from Kelly.

Kelly picked up an empty jar and studied it, trying to think what to say. "You don't have to be afraid of God," she answered finally.

"Well, I know the Bible says He hates sin," Eva said over her shoulder. "My friend—the one who died—told me that all the time. I guess that's why I always think of Him as a judge. I've done a few things He wouldn't exactly approve of."

"But Jesus died to take the punishment for your sins," Kelly said eagerly. "Why don't you—"

"I know what you're going to say. I've heard it a hundred times. No! I'm not going to accept Christ just to get into heaven. Because then I'd have to obey Him and all that." Eva shut the door of the box she'd been working on and leaned over the table to look up at Brutus on his window sill. "I want to live my own life. I'm not ready to belong to anybody," she muttered.

Kelly gazed at her sadly. "You might be miserable, living your own life."

"Maybe. Maybe not," Eva murmured. She stood there, staring out of the window, and in the silence Kelly heard the thump of Tommie's ball hitting the living room floor. It must be almost supper time.

"I'll go start supper," she said. Obviously she wasn't doing any good here.

"Okay." Eva sounded relieved. She swung around and flopped into the armchair. "I'll be there in a couple of minutes," she added, picking up a book.

Kelly climbed the stairs with a heavy heart. Eva knew so much about Christ already. How could she turn away from Him like that?

Tommie was waiting for her in the kitchen, looking hungry. "What's wrong?" she asked, staring at Kelly's face. Kelly tried to smile. "Oh, I've been talking to your sister, that's all. How about macaroni and cheese for supper?"

"Yeah," Tommie agreed. "Make two boxes. I'm starved."

By the time Eva came up to the kitchen, supper was ready. Although Kelly had accidentally put too much milk in the macaroni and cheese, Tommie liked the runny mixture and ate a huge second helping. Eva ate silently and returned to her Den soon afterwards without offering to help; so Kelly dried the dishes for

Tommie. Later she shepherded Tommie from bath to bed, finishing up by reading her a story—about parrots, of course.

Back downstairs in the kitchen, she couldn't help wishing that Dad would come home soon. This big house was kind of creepy when everything was so quiet. Soberly she peered into the empty cookie jar. They'd better start a grocery list.

To cheer herself up, she made her favorite snack: a slice of bread thickly spread with peanut butter and sprinkled with chocolate chips. She took it with her up to the tower. The small room looked cosy in the lamp's soft light, and its blue draperies shut out the gloomy dusk. She curled up on the faded blue cushion of the rocking chair and took a bite of her sandwich. Now was the time to do some serious thinking about this afternoon's visit to the Memorial.

No matter how she tried to explain it away, there was something strange about the way an airplane had landed in the Pines and those boxes had just happened to disappear. Almost as strange as the man, Thurston Grant. Suddenly she remembered what was still bothering her about him: his tattooed eyelids. From what Mr. Carbonell had said, he might be a Marielito.

She began making a mental list: the boxes; the airplane tracks; the Marielitos. And what about the problems at the airport? There had to be some explanation for those too.

She was still puzzling over her list when an idea came, hazily at first, as though it were under a slowly-focusing microscope. Perhaps Thurston Grant was connected to all of this, even to the airport incidents. She considered it, frowning. How could she find out?

The best thing to do would be to tell Dad what she'd discovered. If J. L., his policeman friend, could set up surveillance at that clearing in the Pines, the whole mystery might be solved.

A question wedged itself in her mind: did she really want to solve this mystery? If the airport problems were cleared up, then Dad wouldn't even consider the job back in Missouri. And they'd have to live here forever.

Kelly rocked back and forth so fast that the old chair creaked. How could she give up the hope of going home? She just couldn't.

Her sandwich seemed tasteless now, but she nibbled at it anyway. What I need to do is take a long bath, she told herself abruptly. And I'd better forget about playing detective. There's no point in saying anything at all to Dad.

After her bath she remembered Mr. Carbonell's advice about Bible reading and decided that now would be a good time to start. She settled down on the sofa with her Bible and opened it expectantly.

She read the first chapter of Mark, and then the second and third, surprised at what she was learning about Jesus Christ. These verses described how He'd healed sick people, defeated evil spirits, and commanded men to follow Him. His power was amazing. Anyone who followed Him had better be ready to obey Him. Maybe that's what Eva was talking about.

She stirred uncomfortably on the sofa, fingering the soft leather cover of her Bible. Really, she ought to tell Dad what she had found in the Pines.

No.

She slid the Bible off her lap onto the sofa and stood up. I've got to keep busy, she thought. What about the washing?

She ran downstairs to the washing machine and pulled out the wet laundry. Before she threw the clothes into the dryer, she shook them hard, harder than necessary. She felt about a million miles away from God again. Why had Mr. Carbonell said that He was such a great Friend? She slammed the dryer door shut and raced back up the steps.

What next? She'd put away that Bible, go up to her tower room, and finish moving in. Dad ought to be home from work soon.

It didn't take long to hang up her clothes and fill the small dresser she'd carried up from Eva's room. While she was arranging her books on one of the shelves, she noticed the old embroidery hoop that she and Tommie had found this morning.

She read the crooked little words again and wondered what the rest of the verse said. Impulsively she picked up her Bible and turned to Psalm 28:7.

*The Lord is my strength and my shield; my heart trusted in him, and I am helped–*

*Helped.* Her mind pounced on the word. If anyone needed help, she did. Why didn't God help her?

The page seemed to shimmer before her: *My heart trusted in him. . . .*

She turned away from the verse and took a long time lining up her shoes under the dresser.

I guess I haven't been trusting Him, she finally admitted to herself. I guess I'm afraid of what might happen.

She sprawled across the bed, still arguing with herself. Right here was God's promise that she wouldn't be sorry if she trusted in Him. But trusting wasn't all that easy.

She reached for her Bible and read the verse again, lingering over, *The Lord is my strength and my shield.* "It says He'll make me strong if I trust Him," she murmured, "but why should He care if I trust Him or not?"

She could almost hear Nannette's crisp voice answering: "Because He loves you."

Kelly thought about that love, remembering the warm assurance He'd given when she'd asked for forgiveness only a few days ago. Slowly her resistance melted. She buried her face in the pillow. "Lord, I'm sorry–I've been trying to go my own way again. I do want to obey You; I've got to learn to trust You. But I'll need a lot of help, like You promised."

She fell silent, struggling with despair. At last she whispered, "If You want me to stay here with Dad and not go home, okay. But what about David? I won't ever see him again. I guess that will have to be okay too."

Downstairs, the front door opened and she heard her father's heavy footsteps cross the living room. If she were ever going to talk to Dad, it had to be now. She jumped off the bed and started down the steps.

He was sitting on the sofa reading the newspaper, and he gave her an absent-minded smile when she perched beside him.

"How's everything at the airport?" she began.

"Pretty good. With this warm weather, lots of people are flying. Everything's just about set up for the air show too." He glanced at his paper and back again. "You look tired. Have you been staying up late?"

"No, I'm all right. But Dad, I discovered some things you should know about." After she described the tire tracks in the Pines and the boxes that had disappeared, she told him about the tattoos she'd seen on Thurston Grant.

"Well now, you've been busy, haven't you?" He didn't sound very alarmed. "It's possible, I suppose, that Grant landed out there in the Pines for some reason; probably something connected with his job."

"But what about his tattoos?" she protested. "Maybe he's a Marielito."

He nodded. "Could be. I can't ask him a personal question like that, but maybe J. L. can find out something about his past for me. At least he could check and see if they've got Grant's fingerprints on file." He yawned.

Suddenly Kelly remembered the insect specimens that David had meant for Mr. Taylor. Thurston Grant had probably handled the little plastic boxes. "Wait," she exclaimed. "I have something that might have his fingerprints on it."

She ran upstairs and took David's box from the drawer. Her father looked doubtful when she lifted the cover and showed him the boxes. "Well, I'll see what J. L. thinks." He yawned again. "Meanwhile, I guess it's bedtime for both of us. And don't you worry about any of this. I'll take care of it."

As soon as she woke up the next morning, Kelly began wondering what the police would find out about Thurston Grant. It could take several days, she reminded herself, and she leaned out of the window to admire the view of trees and sky. She wasn't exactly happy this morning, but at least she didn't have the dreadful feeling of aloneness she'd had last night before finding the verse in Psalms.

What was that verse again, anyway? She'd have to memorize it. She pulled the rocking chair close to the window and opened her Bible to Psalm 28:7. Re-reading it, she nodded. The verse sounded just as good this morning as it had last night.

She flipped over to the New Testament and read another chapter in the book of Mark. "Think of it," she told herself happily. "The mighty Jesus who made the demons tremble–He's the very same Lord who is my strength and shield."

When Kelly went out to work at the airport that afternoon, the first thing she wanted to do was talk to Ron. She felt sure that he'd help her investigate Thurston Grant when she told him about the man's tattoos. But Ron was busy working inside an airplane, and she had to be satisfied with watching for the Wren. She was disappointed at how normal everything seemed to be. Maybe she should remind Dad about having J. L. check on Thurston Grant.

She took a set of fuel tickets into his office for him to sign. He looked up with a smile as she laid them on his desk, and asked, "How about getting me a cup of coffee?"

She took his empty cup into the waiting room, but before she could pour his coffee, the phone rang. Dina glanced up from where she was working on the wall chart. "Kelly, can you get that?"

"Sure." Kelly put down the cup, ran back to the counter, and leaned over it to pick up the phone. A few minutes later, after answering the caller's questions about flying lessons, she returned to the coffee maker, where Dina was pouring herself a cup of coffee.

Kelly filled her father's cup, and while she carried it back to him, she tried to think of the best way to bring up the subject of Thurston Grant.

"Did you get a chance to talk to J. L.?" she asked in a low voice.

"Just for a few minutes. Shut the door, will you?" He leaned back in his chair and sipped his coffee. "I've been thinking about the things that have happened around here lately, and it does look like somebody wants to get rid of us. At first I wondered if it could be Luis Carbonell."

"Oh, no," exclaimed Kelly. "I'm sure it's not him."

"I agree. He's a good man," her father said gravely. "Since you're helping me with this project, I might as well tell you that I got another note this morning." He picked up a brown envelope from the pile of mail on his desk. "I'd like to think that this was written by some kids for a prank; I hope they get tired of their games pretty soon."

He took another drink of coffee and slid the brown envelope across the desk toward her. "I was curious about something, though. When was it that you saw those boxes?"

Suddenly he gasped in pain and leaned forward, clutching at his chest. His face flushed red and a film of perspiration stood out on his forehead.

Kelly stared at him. She sprang to the door and flung it open. "Dina, quick! It's Dad–something terrible!"

# Chapter Fourteen
# The Warning

He was sprawled unconscious across his desk, and Kelly ran to put her arms around him. He wasn't breathing. His big, square body felt heavy and lifeless as she fumbled at his wrist, trying to find a pulse.

She could hear Dina on the phone, calling an ambulance. Someone was yelling for Mr. Carbonell, saying something about a heart attack.

In the next minute Luis Carbonell stood beside her. "Let's get him to the floor." He pushed the desk aside, lifted her father down onto the rug, and began working over him while Kelly looked on in helpless terror.

Finally she heard the wail of a siren. Two ambulance attendants ran into the room, and Mr. Carbonell looked up. "The heart is beating again."

"What happened?" one of the men asked. While Kelly stammered an explanation, he prepared to start an IV and attached wires to her father from a black box.

The other man inserted an airway tube and looked at his companion a minute later. "He's not very blue," he said. "Let's go."

They slid her father onto a stretcher and carried him out to the waiting ambulance. As Kelly walked behind them, she stepped over a brown envelope on the floor–the letter her father had been about to show her. Mechanically she picked it up and thrust it into her pocket.

The attendants let her sit in the back of the ambulance, and while they adjusted a green oxygen mask over her father's face, she found his hand. It was limp and cold, but she was thankful to feel the slow, steady beat of his pulse under her fingers. She held his hand tightly as the ambulance rushed down the road with its siren screaming.

At the hospital, the men hurried the stretcher into the emergency room and Kelly scrambled to keep up, only to see them disappear behind a pair of green swinging doors. A nurse gave her some forms to fill out, and she kept making mistakes on them, unable to think about anything except what was happening behind those green doors.

Since she didn't know the number for her father's hospital insurance or his Social Security number, she left those spaces blank, and the nurse told her that she could drop off the information tomorrow.

Tomorrow. Kelly didn't want to think about tomorrow and what it might bring. She crouched on one of the yellow chairs in the waiting room, hardly aware of the shuffling patients and crying babies.

The nurse brought her a message: someone was coming from the airport and wanted her to wait until he got there. Kelly nodded, hoping she wouldn't burst into tears in front of everybody.

When Mr. Carbonell sat down quietly beside her, she couldn't say anything. She gave him a grateful look and kept her eyes on those green doors.

Finally the doors swung open and a tall, white-jacketed man walked briskly toward her. She made herself sit still. "Everything's fine–he's stabilizing," the doctor assured her. "He can't have any visitors, at least not until tomorrow. Why don't you go on home? We'll call you if anything develops."

Kelly didn't like the idea of anything else developing, but she nodded and stood up, her knees shaky with relief.

Mr. Carbonell spoke for the first time. "Well, that's good news. I'll take you home, Kelly."

When they stopped in front of Aunt Jessica's house, he looked at her with concern. "My wife would be glad to come and spend the night with you girls."

Kelly shook her head. "We'll be all right; we're used to managing alone."

"Here's my phone number." He handed her a strip of paper. "Be sure and call if you need anything. I'll pick you up first thing in the morning, yes?"

She nodded, trying to smile her thanks.

Mr. Carbonell's dark eyes met hers. "Remember to talk to the Lord Jesus about this, Kelly. He's the best friend you've got."

That night as she climbed wearily up to her tower room, she remembered his words. At least now she didn't have to be brave and cheerful like she'd tried to be when people asked about Dad and when she'd phoned Mom. She could talk to Someone who understood how scared she'd been today.

She flung herself across the bed and whispered her fears into the pillow. "Oh, Lord, don't let Dad die. Please help him–he needs to know You as his Saviour. And help me to keep trusting You in all this." Once again, she had the assurance of being heard.

Dad is still alive, she reminded herself as she got ready for bed. She had phoned the hospital twice and he was "satisfactory," whatever that meant. Drowsily she repeated the verse that had become her favorite: "*The Lord is my strength and my shield; my heart trusted in him and I am helped. . . .*" Comforted, she fell asleep.

It was still early the next morning when Mr. Carbonell turned into the driveway, but Kelly was waiting for him. Since first opening her eyes, she hadn't been able to think about anything but seeing Dad again.

"He's sleeping," the nurse on duty told them, "so you may take only a peek. Don't waken him."

"He looks pretty good, doesn't he?" whispered Mr. Carbonell. Kelly thought he looked awful–so quiet and pale in the dim room with all those machines attached to him. She nodded stiffly and turned away so no one could see her face.

It wasn't until they were walking back down the long hospital corridor that she thought about the numbers she was supposed to get for the hospital records. She'd have to look for them right away.

Tommie met her at the door, chattering nonstop, and Kelly knew she was trying to cheer her up. Together they washed the dishes and made egg salad sandwiches for lunch. While they ate, Kelly remembered that her father usually kept his important papers in a gray metal box. That would be the place to look for his insurance policy.

She finally found the box in a shelf in his bedroom closet and sat down on the bed to open it. What did an insurance policy look like, anyway? She picked up a handful of papers.

A photograph slid out of a long white envelope and fluttered onto the bedspread. She picked it up idly. It was a picture of her, feeding the chipmunk. Puzzled, she fished in the envelope and found three more pictures of herself: biking; walking in the woods; looking into a store window. How could Dad have taken these photos?

In the bottom of the envelope was a piece of white paper. It had two sentences typed on it:

*Your daughter could be in danger.*
*Go back to Missouri.*

Kelly dropped the paper onto the bedspread with an exclamation of dismay. Was this the unfriendly note Dad had mentioned? No wonder he'd warned her not to go anywhere alone. No wonder he'd been so worried.

With trembling fingers she sorted through the box until she found the insurance papers. While she copied down the numbers she needed, her mind replayed the warning message again and again. Who had sent those pictures? Why?

She stared through the window, reminded of the night she'd caught a glimpse of someone running across the lawn. Had that person been sent to watch her? She shuddered, wondering whether her father had received other notes like this one. Slowly she returned the box to its shelf. What about the brown envelope Dad had started to give her yesterday?

She raced up to the tower room. Her clothes were still on the rocking chair where she'd dropped them last night. Breathlessly, she pulled out the brown envelope. Inside was a piece of rough brown paper that looked as if it had been torn from a grocery bag. She smoothed out its wrinkles and read the typed message: *Today you will receive your last warning: go away!*

Kelly stared at the paper, wondering what it meant. What kind of warning had her father received? It would have been yesterday, she thought. I've got to talk to Dad about this. She glanced at her watch. Good thing Mr. Carbonell would be here soon to take her back to the hospital.

But when Kelly saw her father lying in the hospital bed, she knew she couldn't ask him anything. His face was white and haggard under the gray stubble of his whiskers. He looked as if he were only half awake. She sat down beside the bed and smiled, trying to swallow the lump in her throat. The nurse had warned her not to upset him.

"Everything's going fine," she said brightly.

"Good. I feel better today." He gave her a drowsy smile. "Tomorrow they might even let me eat." His voice dropped to a whisper. "Remember, Kelly, don't go anywhere alone."

"Sure, Dad. I'll stay at home unless I'm working at the airport. Mr. Carbonell has been giving me rides everywhere." She hesitated, then said quickly, "I know the Lord's taking care of me; and I'm praying for you–that you'll get better fast and–and everything. So don't worry." Her father closed his eyes and reached for her hand, gripping it hard.

A minute later the nurse told her to leave, and she found the doctor waiting for her at the end of the hall. After assuring Kelly that her father would be all right, he gave her a quizzical glance.

"It could be," he said, "that your father did not have a typical heart attack. The blood tests suggest that there may be some kind of poison involved."

"Poison?" faltered Kelly.

"Just a possibility." The doctor smiled tranquilly, as if poison were the commonest thing in the world to him. "We'll do some more tests and see what we can find out. Meanwhile, you look like you'd better get some rest."

Kelly walked on slowly to meet Mr. Carbonell in the lobby. So maybe it hadn't been a heart attack after all. Someone might have tried to poison Dad. Was this the warning that the brown note referred to?

As she entered the lobby, Ron Carbonell jumped to his feet and hurried over to join her. "Dad had to go back to the airport; so he told me to give you a ride home," he explained.

"I'm glad," she said. "I have to talk to you." While they walked out to the parking lot, she described the threatening notes her father had received and then told Ron what the doctor had said. "I've got to find out what's going on," she finished, "and I'm hoping you'll help me."

Ron gave her a troubled look as he opened the door of his father's white pick-up. "Why don't you go to the police?"

She shook her head and climbed into the truck. "Dad was looking for some proof. That's what I want to find." She watched him slide behind the steering wheel and noticed the unhappiness on his face. "What's the matter?"

"You know what happened to my sister, Elena?" Ron asked in a husky voice.

Kelly nodded, wondering why he had brought it up.

"And you know that some Marielitos have been seen around here lately? The man who was killed in the Pines last week was one of them."

"I heard about that," she said.

Ron frowned. "Well, my mother has a weak heart. She is very nervous, especially since Elena died. Now she is afraid of these Marielitos–afraid of what will happen. She says we must move."

"Move?" repeated Kelly, unbelieving. "Where to?"

"Another town; another airport south of here. I have to go with her, to take care of her, but my father will keep working here until your dad can get along without him." Ron's eyes were dark with misery. "I don't like it, Kelly. I don't want to leave you, especially with all this trouble."

"When?" She managed to get the word out between stiff lips.

"Sunday. My mother is very determined." He shook his head. "That gives us two days. I'll help you as long as I'm here." He backed the truck out of its parking place, then added, "Don't say anything to Eva about this, okay? I'd better tell her myself."

After Ron dropped her off, Kelly realized that she was so tired she could hardly keep her eyes open. She didn't even feel like figuring out what to do next.

"I'm going to take a nap," she murmured to Eva. "See you later." She stumbled up the stairs, yawning.

When she awoke, morning sunlight was pouring into the tower room. She sat up, still in the clothes she'd worn yesterday, and wished she hadn't missed supper.

Down in the kitchen, Eva greeted her cheerfully. "Well, you sure look a lot better. Fourteen hours of sleep always helps, doesn't it?"

"Sure does. I'm starved." Kelly poured herself a glass of milk. While she scrambled some eggs, Eva lingered in the kitchen. "Did Ron bring you back from the hospital yesterday?" she finally asked Kelly.

"Yes, his dad got tied up at the airport. They sure have been nice to me. I don't know what I'd have done without Mr. Carbonell."

Eva nodded. "He's not as bad as I used to think. Does everything seem to be going okay for your dad?"

"He's getting better, but the doctor thinks someone poisoned him," she said.

Eva looked intrigued. "Really? What kind of poison?"

"They don't know yet." Thoughtfully Kelly asked, "When you lived in Brazil, did you ever hear of a poison that could make it look like someone was having a heart attack?"

Eva nodded. "Sure. There's all kinds of poisons, and some of them have really strange effects. But where would a person around here get it?"

"What if he was a Marielito?" Kelly ate a forkful of eggs, thinking aloud. "He might still have connections with someone in Cuba."

"That makes sense," agreed Eva. "But how can you find out?"

Eva's question echoed in Kelly's mind all morning, even during her visit to the hospital. She had to get some kind of proof. Someone was deadly serious about wanting them to leave.

She gazed at her father's pale face, and her resolution hardened. It was up to her now to find out who had poisoned him, and to prove it. And she had to hurry, before something else happened. If only Ron weren't leaving so soon.

After lunch, Kelly tidied her room and tried to read while she waited for Mr. Carbonell to pick her up again, but the words on the page ran together so that nothing made sense. It was just too hot. She looked outside, and her gaze lingered on the inviting green shade of the tall pines. It would be cool and quiet down there, especially if she sat under the little tree at the edge of the cemetery.

A moment later, she was strolling down the sandy path, her book tucked under her arm. She stepped carefully through the wildflowers and crawled into the shady nook at the base of the tree.

She hadn't been reading for long when the sunlit world beyond her suddenly grew dim. Glancing through the screen of leaves, she discovered that a billowing gray cloud had sailed in front of the sun; dozens more were piling up on the horizon. A thunderstorm must be coming. Good—it might cool things off. But Dad wouldn't like it because the weather would be bad for flying.

Her thoughts wandered to the pilot whose plane had crashed in the Pines during a thunderstorm. She crept out from under the sheltering tree and stretched, watching the dark array of clouds and wishing it was time to leave for the airport.

Maybe the Wren won't be flying tonight because of the weather, she thought. I'd sure like to take a look inside it and maybe find the proof we need. Ron might know if it's back, perhaps in that old barn. This afternoon at work I'll ask him.

## Chapter Fifteen
# Tracking the Wren

At the airport that afternoon, several customers asked Kelly about her father. She answered their questions as well as she could without mentioning the poison and wondered whether any of them were just pretending to be concerned. After filing a stack of bills for Dina, she slipped out to the hangar to find Ron.

He was taking the cowling off the engine of an airplane, and he handed her a paper cup for the screws.

"What're you doing?" she asked.

"Getting ready to change the oil and the filter," he replied. "Did you get any more ideas?"

Kelly shook her head. "I've been wondering if the poison could have come from someone who's a Marielito. Eva thinks it might." Abruptly she changed the subject, "Is the Wren around?"

"No, it left early this morning."

Disappointed, she asked, "Do you have any idea when it'll get back?"

"Not really–wait a minute. It's been flying a lot lately. Let me check something." Ron walked over to study a scheduling chart that hung on the wall. "The Wren's down for a one-hundred-hour inspection first thing Monday morning, so they'll probably try to get back for that.''

Kelly stood still for a minute, trying to think of another plan. If the Wren brought back some more of those boxes and somehow got caught. . . . "Let's see, this is Friday," she said slowly. "Seems like the Wren is usually gone for one or two days. If the plane that lands in the Pines is the Wren, I sure wish I could be there when it gets back–I'm curious about its cargo.''

Ron picked up his screwdriver. "Are you thinking they might bring back some more of your boxes?''

"Yes," she said eagerly. "Do you think it could be tonight?''

Ron shook his head. "Nope. Have you looked outside?''

"Oh, I forgot," Kelly said. "A storm's coming, isn't it?''

"Yes, they're forecasting a line of bad thunderstorms to move in tonight along with those clouds. I doubt that anybody would take a chance on landing out there in this kind of weather.''

He turned back to the engine of the airplane. "How come you're so sure that Thurston Grant and the Wren are doing something illegal?''

"His tattoos. I think he's a Marielito, even if he doesn't look Spanish or anything.''

Ron glanced up sharply. "What tattoos?''

"Remember the tattoos I asked your father about–the ones on a man's eyelids? I saw them on Thurston Grant. It didn't seem important then. I forgot about it until the night after we went to the Memorial. I even told Dad, and he was going to ask J. L. to check on the guy.''

She watched Ron pour a can of oil into the engine. From the look on his face, it seemed that he was listening seriously to her now. "Don't you see: if we could stop the Wren after they've landed with the boxes, that would be proof, wouldn't it?'' she asked. "But how can we keep that airplane on the ground?''

"That's a good question," Ron said. "I could cut the cables for the rudder–they need the rudder for the high performance kind of flying they do. But it's against federal law to damage an airplane.''

"What about letting air out of the tires?"

"Too noisy. They'd notice right away."

Kelly was beginning to feel desperate. "How about putting great big tacks under the tires? Oh–that's dumb."

"Now wait a minute," Ron said patiently, "let me think."

He moved the pan of oil that had drained from the airplane. "I'd better get this out of the way," he said with a grin. "You never know what some people will step into."

She had to smile too, remembering the cup of screws she'd knocked over the first day she'd seen him.

His eyes grew intent. "I know what we could do. See this?" He showed her a small knob on the underside of the engine.

"Yes, what's it for?"

"That's the quick-drain. It's for draining the oil when it needs to be changed, like I'm doing on this airplane. If I push it, then it'll lock open and they'll lose all their oil."

"Doesn't that damage the plane too? "

"Only if the engine's running. They'll see oil all over the ground, and they won't even want to try to start the airplane. They'd know it would wreck the engine."

"But what if the engine cover is on?" Kelly asked.

He had already thought of that. "I'll show you. Give me a couple of screws." Quickly he fastened the bottom half of the engine cowling in place. "See this?" He tapped a little hinged door on the underside of the plane. "It's called a cowl flap. Kneel here and reach up inside. See if you can touch the quick-drain knob."

After a few tries she found the knob; it felt like just a bump under her fingers. She turned to him with growing excitement. "So if you sneak up to the plane and push this, then the oil will leak out? How long before they don't have enough oil to fly?"

"Two to three minutes."

"That's wonderful! Now all we have to do is catch them on the ground." She sobered. "That's all."

"Not easy," Ron agreed, "but maybe we can do it. Looks like my dad's ready to leave. Are you coming with us?"

During her afternoon visit to the hospital, Kelly learned that her father had improved enough to come home the next day. The blood tests confirmed that a small amount of some unknown poison had caused his symptoms.

Kelly brooded while she washed the supper dishes. Where had the poison come from? It had to be connected with the person who had sent those threatening notes.

Thurston Grant? He could have taken the pictures of her. She'd noticed his camera the first time she saw him. And Tommie had seen him with a camera last Sunday. A scientist might use a camera too, though. Kelly's thoughts circled dizzily. And if Tommie saw him on Sunday, and the Wren was away that day, who had been flying it?

A rumble of thunder made her glance out of the window. The storm that had been threatening all afternoon broke over the house at last. Lightning split the blackened sky again and again, thunder grumbling after it, and Kelly was glad not to be out in the Pines. Surely the Wren would not fly back tonight.

Up in her room, she was working on a letter to David when she heard a timid knock. "Come in," she called, raising her voice above the pounding rain.

Tommie's curly head appeared around the corner. Her brown eyes looked troubled.

"You're not afraid of the storm, are you?" asked Kelly in surprise.

"Nah, not me." Tommie hesitated, then held out the tract Kelly had given her. "I took good care of it for you. It tells how that boy asked Jesus to be his Saviour. Do you think Jesus would be my Saviour too?"

Kelly's heart lifted. She smiled. "Sure. The Bible says that He died for all of us. I asked Him to be my Saviour one day too."

"Were you happy? Did He really forgive your sins?"

"Yes, He really did forgive me, and then I was happy. But it's a quiet sort of happiness–not like fireworks exploding."

"Well, what do I have to do?" asked Tommie.

"First, you tell Him you're sorry for your sins," Kelly said, remembering what she had done. "Then you thank Him for dying on the cross and taking your punishment. Then you just tell the Lord Jesus that you want Him to be your Saviour."

She put an arm around Tommie's thin shoulders. "It's like getting a present from someone. All you have to do is take it and say 'thank you.' "

Tommie nodded and closed her eyes. "Dear God, I'm sorry for all the bad things I did, 'specially the thing about the key. And Jesus, thank You for dying for me. And please, I want You to be my Saviour."

She looked up at Kelly. "Is that all?"

Kelly hugged her. "That's all. Now you belong to Him." She stood up and looked through the book shelves behind them. "I saw a Bible here somewhere. No one will mind if you use it. Here, I'll mark John 3:16 for you. Let's read it again together."

It wasn't until much later that night as she was drifting off to sleep, that Kelly wondered about the key Tommie had mentioned in her prayer. Why had she been so sorry about a key?

First thing the next morning, Eva suggested that since Kelly's father was coming home that day, they should celebrate. "Let's make him a cherry pie," she exclaimed.

"Sure, if you show me how." Kelly was glad to find her in such a friendly mood. "I'll make the one for Dad. You can make one for Ron," she added with a grin.

Eva blushed, but all she said was, "We'll have to get started if we want to be done on time."

By imitating everything Eva did, Kelly managed to roll out her own pastry and cook the cherry filling. When she finally took her bubbling pie out of the oven, she sniffed happily at the fragrant aroma. "Smells great," she said. "And it looks delicious. I actually did it!"

They finished cleaning up the kitchen just as Mr. Carbonell arrived with Kelly's father. She was dismayed to see how sick he still looked. Slowly he climbed the porch steps; then he sank onto the sofa with an exhausted sigh. After Mr. Carbonell left, Tommie asked, "Do you want lunch? We made you something special: a cherry pie."

"That's very nice." Kelly's father leaned back and closed his eyes. "I think I'll just have some soup for now."

As they walked back to the kitchen, Eva murmured, "Never mind, it'll keep until he's feeling better." Reluctantly Kelly put her pie into the refrigerator.

By the time Kelly's father had finished his soup, he was yawning. "I think I'd better get some sleep," he said. "Kelly, could you and Tommie take this letter out to the airport for me? I forgot to give it to Luis this morning. It's about the air show next week, and Dina needs to type it up right away."

"I don't like leaving you alone," Kelly began, but Eva spoke up quickly.

"I'll be here all afternoon in case the phone rings. Then when Tommie gets back, I'll bring that pie out to the airport for Ron."

Kelly could see that she didn't know yet about Ron's plans to leave. He'd better hurry up and tell her. Poor Eva; she was going to be really upset.

At the airport, everything seemed to be running as usual, although Dina looked worried and sat tapping her foot nervously while she answered the phone.

There was plenty for Kelly to do. She managed to concentrate fairly well until a pilot walked past her with a cup of steaming coffee. The rich smell of the coffee started an idea churning in her head. What about the coffee that Dad drank just before he got sick? Could someone have slipped the poison into his cup when she'd left it to answer the phone? It could have been just a few drops of a colorless liquid.

Kelly looked around the waiting room, wondering how it might have been done.

From where she sat by the telephone, the only way she could see the coffee maker was by leaning over the counter. And Dad couldn't see it at all from his office. She couldn't remember who had been taking a coffee break when she'd left his cup there by the coffee maker. It could have been anyone. She went back to her work with a sigh.

She had almost finished when Eva arrived with the cherry pie and disappeared into the hangar. A short time later, Ron carried the pie out to Mr. Carbonell's truck. Kelly watched through the big airport window as he explained something to Eva. Was he telling her that he had to move? Eva's face was turning red, like it did when she got angry. Finally she whirled away from Ron and jumped onto her bicycle.

After work, Kelly went out behind the hangar to talk to Ron. He looked unhappy, but he didn't say anything about Eva. Instead, he remarked, "Looks like good flying weather tonight." He gave her a level glance. "You want to go for a walk later on?"

Her pulse quickened. "Sure."

In a low voice he added, "I've been thinking about those boxes. Before we do anything drastic, I'd like to take another look around the clearing. And since we don't know exactly when the plane's coming in, we'd better make sure we're there right after dark."

"Okay," Kelly agreed.

"You want to meet me at the fire tower?"

"I can't go anywhere alone," she reminded him.

"Then I'll come pick you up," he said. "It's a long hike; hope we get there before they do."

When Kelly arrived at Aunt Jessica's house, she found Tommie sitting on the porch swing, looking downcast. "What's for supper?" she asked Tommie after Mr. Carbonell had driven off.

"I don't know. I guess you'll have to make it," Tommie said glumly. "Eva's mad about something."

"Don't worry, we won't starve." Kelly tried to cheer her up. "How about creamed snails on toast?"

Tommie gave her a small grin. "Or pancakes?"

"Pancakes," agreed Kelly. "We can have a salad too."

While they made the pancakes, Kelly noticed that Tommie still looked upset. Finally she asked, "Are you worried about Eva? You know, she's really unhappy. I've been praying for her."

Tommie nodded. "Yes. She's so smart, and everything, but I guess she needs Jesus. I can pray for her too. But there's something else." Tommie's lower lip quivered. She was as close to tears as Kelly had ever seen her. "I did something wrong."

"Want to tell me about it?"

"You'll hate me, but I've got to, even though I know God's forgiven me." She chewed on a fingernail. "The key–I stole it for Eva and she–oh, I'm sorry!"

"What key?"

"The extra key for your dad's new locks. We heard him say he'd keep it in his car, and Eva got me to take it for her. Then she put it back later."

Kelly stared at her. "What did she want it for?"

"Well, that's how she got into the hangar and sprayed that white stuff on the airplane."

"Why in the world would Eva do a thing like that?"

"I think she wanted to get Mr. Carbonell in trouble." Kelly gave her a puzzled glance and Tommie explained. "She was mad at him because he found her walking around in the Pines and warned her not to go out there alone. I guess she was afraid he'd tell Mrs. York."

Tommie sighed, adding, "When your aunt said Mr. Carbonell had been in prison, Eva got the idea of doing things at the airport so he'd get blamed. But lately she doesn't seem to hate him so much."

Kelly stacked pancakes on a plate and tried to fit this new information into the puzzle. "Did Eva cut the tie-down ropes on Saturday too?"

"Probably. She said she had some more plans. I think she did that stuff when she went out in the middle of the night, but I guess she decided to stop after she got to know Ron."

"Yes, that makes sense," murmured Kelly. "I know she's changed her mind about Mr. Carbonell, and it's probably because of Ron. I've got to talk to her. I hope she comes down for supper."

But Eva did not appear, and the hours inched by until Kelly's father went to bed. Restlessly she watched the daylight fade, wondering how smart it was to go into the Pines tonight. If anything happened to her and Ron, no one would even know where they had gone. Tommie was too young to be given such a responsibility, and she didn't want to say anything to Dad unless it was absolutely necessary. The only person left was Eva.

Kelly hesitated in front of the closed bedroom door, then finally knocked. When Eva opened it, her face was dark and unfriendly. She listened in silence while Kelly explained what she and Ron were going to do.

"If I'm not back after a couple of hours," Kelly added, "I need you to wake up Dad and have him phone J. L. and maybe Mr. Carbonell. Tell them we've gone out to the Memorial."

"Why should I?" asked Eva sullenly. "I'm not even sure I believe you. Maybe this is just a cover-up and you're going on a date with Ron." Ignoring Kelly's protest, she burst out, "Oh, why does he have to move anyway? It's all your fault that he's leaving."

"Now you listen to me," Kelly said. "I don't care about another boy in the world besides David. Ron is just helping me because his sister was killed by the Marielitos. Remember: if someone doesn't call the police in time, Ron might get hurt too."

Eva glared at her, picked up a hairbrush, and turned pointedly away.

Kelly left her and went to settle Tommie into bed, trying not to feel discouraged. It looked as if Eva wasn't going to be much help tonight. Just in case everything went wrong, she left a note on her dresser, although probably no one would find it until tomorrow morning.

She dressed in dark clothes and hurried out to the front porch, where Ron was waiting. After she checked to make sure she had a tire patch kit, they began the long bike trip in silence.

Just past the airport, Ron turned onto a small, twisting road that Kelly had never used before. The slender moon cast a pale glow across their way, but it could not penetrate the forest, which rose like a dark wall on either side of them. Kelly kept her mind off the gloomy pine woods and the endless miles by trying to untangle the events that had led up to this night.

Tommie's confession helped to explain two of the airport incidents. The police seemed to think that the bearded man they questioned had set the smoke bomb. But why? And who had stolen the radio? Did Thurston Grant know anything about it?

When the road petered out, becoming a path filled with loose sand, they hid their bikes in the bushes and continued on foot. The path seemed like a dark tunnel into the deepest part of the woods, and Kelly found herself listening uneasily to the half-heard whisperings of the trees.

A faint rustling–or was it a footstep?–startled her. She turned quickly and glimpsed a small shadow.

"Tommie, what are you doing here?" she exclaimed under her breath.

Tommie ran up and clung to her arm. "I had to ask you something; so I went up to your room, then I saw your note. I know where you're going. Please let me come," she begged.

Kelly looked at Ron. He shrugged. "I guess we'll have to take her along." To Tommie, he said sternly, "Be very quiet. We're getting closer."

He turned off the flashlight he'd been using, and they slipped silently past the Memorial, heading for the old cellar hole. When they reached the edge of the clearing, Ron paused, scanning it carefully. "Okay," he said at last. "Let's see about those boxes."

Kelly ran to the pile of ruins. For a minute she thought the hole was empty, but after she lifted off a covering of branches, she saw the bulky outlines of several boxes.

They looked like cardboard cartons. In the pale moonlight she could read the writing stamped across the side of each one: *S&S GARDEN CENTER.*

"Come on," whispered Tommie excitedly.

Before Kelly could stop her, she squeezed down into the hole and pulled out her pocketknife.

"Hey, what're you doing?" asked Ron.

"I'll be careful. I can slip this blade right under the tape and pull off one side of it," Tommie said without looking up.

Kelly leaned down and helped open up the flaps of the box.

Ron shielded the flashlight with his hand as he shone it into the box. He grunted in surprise.

"Pine cones?" Kelly brushed aside a layer of pine cones and uncovered a brown plastic squirrel and a plump plastic duck. "Lawn ornaments? I can't believe this."

"Well, now we know," Ron said.

"Some treasure," muttered Tommie.

Kelly frowned at the plastic squirrel and picked it up. It was heavier than she'd expected. She turned it over and pushed it back down into the pine cones. In the beam from Ron's flashlight, she saw that two holes had been drilled in its base, but she didn't have time to wonder about that, for Tommie was whispering to her and Ron had switched off his light.

"Want to open another box?" asked Tommie.

"No," Ron said. "We've got to get out of here."

With a start Kelly realized that they could get into a lot of trouble for what they'd done. In frantic haste she helped Tommie close the flaps and smooth the tape into place. Then, while Tommie scrambled out of the hole, she rearranged the dried branches. They ran for the covering darkness of the woods.

Once they were back in the trees, Kelly waited uneasily for a comment from Ron. But all he did was ask casually, "Do you still want to go see if the Wren comes in?"

"Yes," she said in a small voice, "though I can't imagine why they have to make such a big secret about a cargo of garden stuff."

"I've seen the van for that garden store out in the Pines a couple of times," said Ron thoughtfully.

"Me too," murmured Kelly. They walked single file down the path, Ron leading the way. Kelly trailed behind him, wondering how he could see anything and wishing she hadn't brought him out on this useless hike. The flopping of Tommie's shoe laces distracted her.

She stopped. "Tie those laces, will you?" she whispered.

Tommie bent over her shoes, and while Kelly waited she caught a whiff of something acrid in the pine-scented air. Cigarette smoke? Had Ron noticed it?

Before she could call ahead to him, she saw a dark shadow lunge at Ron from the trees.

There was only time to see that Ron was down, that his attacker was huge. She reached for Tommie and ducked into a thicket of bushes. Crouching there, she trembled as she listened to the scuffling sounds on the path.

# Chapter Sixteen
# Night Flight

"Come on!" Tommie was whispering in her ear. "They'll look for us next."

Not daring to protest, Kelly crept after her through the darkness, conscious only of the strangled silence behind them. What was happening to Ron?

After a safe interval she asked, "Do you know where you're going?"

The curly head nodded. "Yes. There's a couple of deer trails that lead past the Memorial. One of them is just ahead of us." She pointed through the trees.

"What about Ron?" fretted Kelly. "I hate to run off and leave him."

"And get caught too?" answered Tommie. As they felt their way through the underbrush, she asked, "Do you think we ought to go home?"

"Not yet," said Kelly. "This whole set-up is strange. Whoever grabbed Ron must be doing something wrong out here. Let's keep going."

A few minutes later they saw the sandy surface of a trail glimmering through the trees. Kelly heard soft, hurried footsteps coming toward them, and paused warily in the bushes.

It was only Dina, walking quickly and carrying her brown leather flight bag. Kelly gave a sigh of relief and started forward.

The moonlight glinted on Dina's blonde hair and on the thermos in her hand. Kelly froze, remembering, "Coffee—can't fly without it." Dina always said that.

A chill sliced along her spine. Where was Dina flying tonight?

Kelly touched Tommie's arm and they dropped to the ground. Dina must be part of this too, she thought unhappily.

Dina and her coffee. . . . Kelly had a sudden and terrible suspicion. Was it Dina who had slipped something into Dad's cup while Kelly was on the phone? Now she remembered that Dina had been working on the wall chart that morning, right next to the coffee maker.

Kelly whispered her suspicions to Tommie, then asked, "You said there was another trail?"

"Yes, but we'll have to circle 'way around. Hurry."

As soon as they found the other trail, Tommie started off at a fast trot. Kelly followed her blindly through the endless dark pines, trying not to listen to the panic that was beginning to whimper inside her. Even if they got to the Memorial in time, should she try to stop the plane? Could she do it by herself?

Tommie slowed down as they neared the parking lot by the Memorial. She slipped a small hand into Kelly's. "Aren't you scared? I am. Can Jesus help us?"

Kelly bit her lip. She had forgotten about the Lord: forgotten again. She squeezed Tommie's hand. "Yes, He can," she whispered. "He even gave me a promise. Listen: *The Lord is my strength and my shield; my heart trusted in him and I am helped.*"

"That's good. I feel better already," Tommie whispered back.

So do I, thought Kelly. "Lord Jesus," she prayed silently, "I need Your help tonight. Show me what to do, and make me brave enough to do it."

They hurried on, and soon they could hear the roar of an airplane. "Here they come! We just made it," Kelly murmured. As it passed overhead, the Wren gleamed silver in the moonlight, looking like a great luminous bird.

They ran through the trees, heading for the edge of the parking lot, and Kelly wondered why a car was parked near the big clearing behind the Memorial. When its headlights flicked on, she realized that the plane was going to use the clearing as a landing strip, and the car was lighting it for them.

The Wren landed smoothly on the gravel and taxied close to the trees. Kelly recognized Thurston Grant right away when he jumped out of the plane and opened the baggage compartment. Dina emerged from the trees, and the two of them slowly lifted a box out of the plane and carried it off into the darkness.

Kelly's breath caught in her throat at the sight of their efficient operation. She had to stop the Wren from leaving.

"What are you going to do?" Tommie whispered.

"Something Ron told me about. If I can. Then we've got to get to a phone."

"Thurston Grant's cabin?" suggested Tommie. "I know a short cut that goes near it."

"Okay, good." Kelly studied the airplane. On the underside of its nose she could see the part that Ron had called a cowl flap. The baggage compartment opened on the far side of the plane, close to the trees. If they went back into the woods with another box, there was a chance that she could get to the Wren and open the quick-drain without getting caught. But she'd have to go all the way across the parking lot to do it.

She could feel the quick, suffocating beat of her heart, and she took a long breath to steady herself. "Wait here," she whispered to Tommie.

She crept soundlessly across the gravel, feeling as conspicuous in her dark clothes as a rabbit on a field of snow. When at last she reached the towering shadow of the Memorial, she clung to its rough surface and waited for them to make another trip back into the trees.

As soon as they left, she darted to the nose of the airplane. She could feel the engine's heat through the metal skin of the plane; it was surprisingly hot. A warning rang in her head: if she touched the wrong part inside there, she'd get burned.

She knelt on the gravel, reaching carefully–*carefully*–up into the cowl flap. Where was the knob? There.

She pushed it, felt hot oil on her fingers, and recoiled. Not good enough. Again she reached in, bracing herself for the oil, and pushed hard. This time she felt it snap into place. She turned and sprinted back to the Memorial. After a quick check of the woods, she made another breathless dash across the parking lot. By the time she reached the sheltering trees, oil was already making a dark, spreading puddle on the gravel under the airplane.

She wiped her oily fingers on a handful of leaves and gasped, "Okay now, let's get to that cabin and phone the police."

It was a longer distance to the cabin than she'd remembered, and the precious minutes were slipping away fast. "Hurry, hurry," she told herself, ignoring the stitch of pain in her side. If the police didn't get there soon, Grant might do something else with the boxes.

What in the world was so important about those boxes? And the way they had lifted them so carefully out of the airplane–it just didn't make sense. A small, separate corner of her brain gnawed on that question as she ran down the trail.

When the shadowy outline of the cabin's roof came into sight, she made herself slow down and take a good look at it. Her heart sank. Someone else was using Thurston Grant's cabin.

She crouched in the bushes and scowled at the thin, bearded man who sat smoking on the front steps. Behind him on the porch lay a still figure. Could that be Ron?

"I'm going in the back door," she said to Tommie in an urgent whisper. "I've got to get to that phone. If something happens to me, go to the airport and phone the police from there; break a window if it's the only way to get in."

Tommie nodded solemnly. Kelly crept past the silent cabin and paused in the trees behind it. The back door was only a few yards away. But as she started toward it, a hand clamped over her mouth and a muscled arm pulled her back.

"Keep quiet, and I'll let you go," whispered a voice in her ear.

She squirmed desperately against the man, intending to run as soon as he released her. Then she saw his face in the dim light and recognized his uniform. "J. L.–"

His hand smothered her glad cry. He gave her a shake. "Hey–keep quiet. Thurston Grant might be in there."

She shook her head at him, mumbling under his hand until he took it away, her words tripping over each other as she told him what had happened and her suspicions about the Marielitos.

"Your dad told me what you'd noticed about Grant. And we did get a few fingerprints off those boxes. His real name is Paulos Ramirez. That's why we're watching him tonight." J. L. pulled out a small walkie-talkie and muttered into it.

After listening intently, he said to Kelly, "They're on their way already–they're almost to the Memorial. Someone told your dad that you'd gone out there."

Eva! She'd changed her mind. And it was a good thing she'd told Dad so soon. They just might get there in time to catch Thurston Grant.

J. L. put away the walkie-talkie. "We're going to close in, since you're sure Grant isn't here. Now stay put. I don't want this other guy taking any hostages."

"He's got Ron," she reminded him.

"Just let me do my job, will you?" He gave her a quick smile and faded into the shadows.

Moments later, Kelly saw another figure slipping along the side of the house. She heard a surprised grunt from the man on the steps. After a long silence, lights went on inside the house.

"You can come and get your friend, Kelly," called J. L.

She ran to the thicket where she had left Tommie, and they joined the two policemen on the porch. Ron was sitting up, rubbing his wrists. While the other policeman finished untying Ron's feet, the thin man jangled his handcuffs and watched, looking worried.

"What happened?" asked Ron. "Did you stop them?"

J. L.'s walkie-talkie crackled, and Kelly stiffened as he bent to listen to it. "He says there's a box still on the plane . . . they're checking. . ." A moment later J. L. gave her a puzzled look. "All they can find is pine cones and garden supplies."

"There's got to be something else, maybe inside one of those plastic things. Something valuable," Kelly exclaimed. When J. L. spoke into the walkie-talkie again, the handcuffed man jerked to his feet. She took a closer look at him. "I've seen this man before," she said. "He drives a white van that says S&S GAR-DEN CENTER, like on those boxes."

J. L. was listening again to the walkie-talkie. "Got it." He grinned at Kelly. "Those lawn ornaments were hollow. And they found birds hidden in there. Parrots, to be exact."

Tommie jumped up with an excited yip. "Parrots, huh?"

J. L. faced the handcuffed man. "Where did those parrots come from?"

The man shrugged. "Maybe Florida," he mumbled.

J. L. gave him a stern look. "You might as well be helpful because we've been watching you guys for a long time and this whole operation is going to break wide open."

The man stared at him for a minute, then lowered his eyes. "Birds from Mexico, I think."

"Where were they going?"

"Today I drive to New York. Sometimes Newark. Sell there for a lotta dollars."

J. L. nodded. "That's your van, back in the trees?"

"Yeah."

J. L. started into the cabin, then paused. "Apparently the girl–Dina–takes turns flying the plane. From the charts she had, it looked like she was going to take the plane to another drop-off point. I wonder if Grant was running the whole show."

Now the handcuffed man was eager to talk. "Yes–Grant is the boss here. I tell you everything and you help me too? I only made that smoke bomb because Grant said to. It was part of the plan."

"What plan?" asked J. L.

"The bosses in New York who send Grant down here say they want to use this airport for their business. They don't want a man like Jonson here; so they try to get him to leave, like the other one did."

"Was Grant handling the flights too?"

"Yeah. He has a radio, a special one–he had Juan make some kind of adapter for it–and he tells us what to do and talks to the airplane with it."

Ron pulled himself stiffly to his feet. "That sounds like our stolen radio." He limped into the cabin, Kelly behind him, and stopped at a room off the kitchen. After examining a small black box on the cluttered desk he remarked, "Yes, that's Mr. Biltner's radio, all right. See where the back corner is chipped? I remember noticing that when I worked on it."

Kelly was looking out the window. "There comes a Jeep. What's happening?"

From the porch, she and Ron watched J. L. talking to the driver of the Jeep. Finally they took the handcuffed man to the Jeep and had him get in the back seat. As it drove off, a police van pulled up to the cabin, and a policeman jumped out.

"Come on, kids, we'll give you a ride," said J. L.

Kelly started to climb into the van and stopped short. "Dad!" she cried. "You should be home in bed."

"Not when my daughter is out running around in the Pines," he said gruffly. Then he grinned, and she knew he wasn't as angry as he sounded.

She smiled at Mr. Carbonell, not surprised to see him there too. It was just like him to come along in case Dad needed help.

"This is a good break for us," J. L. said as he drove slowly down the road. "We've wanted to get a handle on these guys for a long time. Who'd have ever guessed they were smuggling birds?"

"What happens next?" asked Ron.

J. L. wore a grin on his freckled face. "I think we can convince the driver of that white van to help us out. We'll let him deliver those birds to New York so we can take a good look at S&S Garden Center, if there is such a place."

"Why would anyone go to all this trouble to smuggle parrots into New York?" asked Kelly.

"There's plenty of money in it, for one thing," J. L. observed. "Take those parrots we found tonight. There's a lot of restrictions on bringing them into the country because they're so rare. They also carry contagious diseases."

The young policeman added, "Luis was telling me about some smuggling operations he's heard of." He turned to Mr. Carbonell. "You said some guys might pay only five dollars apiece to get the birds smuggled across the border from Mexico?"

Mr. Carbonell nodded, and J. L. went on, "Then they use a small plane for quick transportation up north to places like New York where people have the money to pay for an exotic pet. Some macaws sell for thousands of dollars."

Tommie made a face. "I sure found that out," she said. "But don't the birds die on the way?"

J. L. frowned. "Plenty of them do–that's why the smugglers have to work fast. The birds are drugged, their beaks are taped shut, and then they get stuffed into all kinds of hiding places. Those lawn ornaments had openings in them so the birds could get air, but they wouldn't last more than a couple of days."

"Poor things!" exclaimed Tommie indignantly. Kelly nodded at her in agreement.

"And something else," J. L. said, "we're noticing that there's often a connection between the wild-bird trade and other kinds of smuggling. I wouldn't be surprised to find out that this is a sideline to a big drug operation. That's why we want to follow the trail for a while longer."

"Good idea," agreed Kelly's father. "It must be a pretty big operation if they wanted to get control of the airport."

"Did Grant admit what he was doing?" asked Ron.

"Won't say a word without his lawyer there, but his men are already saying plenty and they sound scared. Apparently he had a shoot-out with one of them last week and got wounded himself. The man he shot was that body we found in the Pines.''

"What about Dina?'' asked Kelly softly.

"She was ready to talk. It sounds like she didn't realize what she was getting into until it was too late,'' remarked J. L. "She admitted putting something into your dad's coffee cup, though. Grant got the stuff from his Marielito friends and blackmailed her into using it.''

"I'll be sorry to lose her in spite of everything,'' Kelly's father said. "She's a good pilot.''

Quietly Ron asked, "So this was all a Marielito set-up?''

"Looks like it,'' J. L. answered. "We've been watching them operate on a small scale for quite a while. Seems like they got greedy; so they sent Grant down here this summer to oversee an expansion program.''

He glanced back at Kelly's father and chuckled. "Trouble was they needed an airport to operate from. Dina was helpful, but they didn't like the looks of Mr. Jonson here.''

"No wonder Grant wanted me to leave,'' said Kelly's father. "Him and his threatening letters! I was beginning to think that we might be better off in Missouri after all.'' He rested his head on the back of the seat and smiled. "Now maybe we'll have some peace around the airport for a while.''

Kelly leaned against him with a smile of her own. The Lord had kept His promise–He'd really helped her tonight. They wouldn't be going back to Missouri; she knew that now. She'd have to write and tell David how his insect boxes had helped out. *Oh, David. . . .* Firmly she closed her mind to those thoughts. The Lord would still be with her–*here*–and He'd be a strong Friend.

The police van stopped at the Carbonells' house first. "Thanks for coming along, Luis,'' said Kelly's father. He smiled at Ron. "I guess this will be good news for your mother, won't it?''

Ron grinned. "Sure enough. See you later.''

As they drove on, Kelly said, "I'm glad Eva told you where we went tonight.''

"Yes, she was worried about you going into the Pines," her father said. "She broke down and said that it was partly her fault, something about pulling some pranks at the airport."

"Tommie told me about that today," Kelly answered. "And after I thought about it, things began to fit together better than when I was trying to blame the Marielitos for everything."

When they got home, Eva met them with an anxious face. Kelly smiled at her. "Thanks, Eva. You saved the day, or the night–whatever that expression is! Tommie will tell you all about it. I'll be back down in a couple of minutes. I've got to help Dad."

She followed close behind his shaky progress up the stairs. He was looking very white again. He sank into the armchair in his room and closed his eyes.

After a moment he said, "I did some thinking while I was in the hospital, Kelly. I'm sorry about the problems between me and your mother. I guess I've been pretty stubborn about wanting my own way. So has she."

He gave her a tired smile. "You said something about praying. Maybe that's a good idea. Anyway, I shouldn't have left you out of what was going on." He sighed, then continued, "Meanwhile, I guess it's not fair to expect you to leave your school and your friends and start a whole new life out here with me."

He paused again, and Kelly made herself sit still, waiting. "So I've agreed to let you go back to Missouri if you want to. There's no hurry. Just let me know when you make up your mind."

He fumbled with the sunglasses in the case on his belt, took them out, and polished them with his handkerchief. His face was turned away from her, as if he were unconcerned. But she could see the knotted muscles in his jaw and knew that he cared.

She watched him, thinking that there really wasn't anything to decide. That night in the tower room, when she'd told the Lord that she'd do what He wanted, she had made her choice. She knew now that Dad needed her and she needed him.

She picked up his hand, thankful to feel it warm and strong as his fingers closed over hers. Remembering how tired he was, she kept her tone light. "I'm not going anywhere, Dad. You need someone to take care of you."

He cleared his throat. "Well, I'm glad for that." He sat up a little straighter in his chair. "I do have some good news. I've found someone to stay with you girls."

"Who?"

"Nannette's going to visit us for a while."

"Oh, wonderful!" Kelly exclaimed.

"And since the air show is coming up next week," he added, "I'll need an extra line boy at the airport. So I asked her to bring along some help–just any kid she knew that might be useful around airplanes."

He grinned at her, obviously pleased with himself.

Kelly's heart caught painfully in her throat. "David?" she whispered. "David's coming?"

"He sure is. You and Eva will have someone else to bake pies for."

She stared at him, and everything started to blur.

His pleased grin wavered. "Why, honey, aren't you glad?"

"Glad? Oh, yes I'm glad! If only you knew–" She brushed away her tears, and then leaned down to hug him.